THAT WILDER MAN

SUE PHILLIPS

Sweetbriar Creek Publishing Company
PO Box 92683
Henderson, NV 89014-8845

https: www.SuePhillipsAuthor.com

Publisher's Note: This is a work of fiction. Names, characters, places, and incidents are a product of the author's imagination. Locales and public names are sometimes used for atmospheric purposes. Any resemblance to actual people, living or dead, or to businesses, companies, events, institutions, or locales are completely coincidental.

PRINTING HISTORY
Harlequin Temptation #652 Harlequin Books S.A. / May 1997
Sweetbriar Creek Publishing Company / Print version October 2019

Book Cover Design © 2016 HotDamnDesigns.com

IN HONOR OF

Sam Roberts of Alton, Illinois and the many volunteers who helped their neighbors during the "Great Flood of '93."

SPECIAL THANKS TO

Julie Hurwitz of the 1993 RWA Conference Committee, for the adventure on Sunday, August 1, 1993 that inspired this story.

Larry Williams, who inspired the character of Max "Wildman" Wilder. When I wrote this book, I had no idea the story would be so similar to our lives after we went our separate ways. I wish you love and happiness.

Mindy Neff, Sandra Paul, Jackie Radoumis and **Louzana Kaku**—my *Artist's Way* buddies. I love you all!

IN MEMORY OF

Don Phillips, my husband of forty-two years—Thank you for believing in me. I miss you forever.

CHAPTER 1

Six-point-nine-million dollars doled out over twenty years was around $226,000 a year, give or take a thousand, after Uncle Sam got his share.

Six years after he won the California lottery, Max Wilder still enjoyed watching curious folks go bug-eyed by the numbers. He had waited until that first check was in his hands before he had quit his piloting job of flying corporate execs around in private jets. Then he left Los Angeles behind and relocated to Phoenix. Sometimes, he still had a hard time adjusting to the scope of it all.

That's not to say he didn't like what the money could do. Like right now. If somebody had told him six years ago that one day he would be rich enough to fly emergency supplies to the Midwest for flood victims, he would've laughed them off the Learjet he piloted for Corporate-Air, the Los Angeles-based private airline and his employer at the time.

Yet here he was, sitting in the pilot's seat of his own vintage Beech-17, hauling cases of rubber gloves and boots, flashlights and batteries, and a slew of other things needed by the disaster-relief agency. This trip to Texas was the last out-of-state run to the cities where volunteers had accumulated donations. Max was bone-tired, but he didn't mind. The job of white knight was a lot easier than he thought it would be. After the adrenaline high of his first mercy mission, he was hooked.

With the loud engines droning in his ears, Max gazed out his window at the Mississippi River. He was only a few miles from the convergence with the Missouri. No matter how many times he flew over the flooded areas, he would never get used to seeing the murky water spread out in all directions across the flat plain. It was as bad as the Great Flood of '93 and a few others since then. Only this one looked as though it might be the granddaddy of them all, swallowing up more farmland, more small towns. He could make out dots of treetops and white farmhouses, some of the latter submerged to their roofs. In the middle of the watery landscape, Max spotted parallel green lines that looked more like toy railroad tracks than the original tree-lined riverbank.

It was a hell of a helpless feeling watching that river rise day after day, week after week, threatening the land his family had farmed for generations. Good thing none of them were around to see the devastation. They were gone—his grandparents, his old man, his mother.

Even Johnny.

The aerial view blurred from the moisture in Max's eyes. With a shake of his head to clear his vision, he turned his attention back to flying, refusing to believe that his fuzzy eyesight sprang from any emotional response. Too many hours in the air had finally caught up with him. As soon as he delivered these supplies into Saint Louis, he was going to head back to Alton and hit the sack for at least three days straight.

He couldn't let himself think about Johnny McKenzie. But the more he tried to block the memories of his friend, the more they hounded him. Somewhere in the deepest recesses his mind, Max had thought that someday, somehow, he would find it in his heart to forgive Johnny. He had always thought there would come a time when he would come home to Alton and bury the hatchet.

That time ran out two years earlier, when Max had gotten the news in a roundabout way that Johnny had been on the fatal flight of a commercial airline. Max had wanted to attend the funeral. He'd even made it as far as the United Methodist Church, only to pull up short at the sight of Liza Jane. Before she could spot him, he had ducked out of sight.

Liza Jane Brown... No, not Brown.

Her name had been McKenzie for too many years now, Max reminded himself. Liza Jane *McKenzie*. Damn, how the mere thought of her married name could still slug him in the gut, even after sixteen years.

Max glanced down at the instrument panel, then out the window at the waterscape below. In a few more minutes, he'd be landing in Saint Louis. Another hour and he'd be back in Alton where he could lay low at the old farmhouse until the next mercy mission. With any luck, he would avoid going any place he might bump into Liza Jane. He couldn't allow himself to see her again. He couldn't look down into her green eyes without letting her see the scars of hurt, of pain, of betrayal. He couldn't risk asking the question that had haunted him for so long—*why did you choose Johnny instead of me, Liza Jane?*

~

MAX IS BACK.

Standing on the steps of the ancient McKenzie boarding house overlooking the swollen Mississippi, Elizabeth McKenzie couldn't stop thinking of Max Wilder. Two weeks had passed since she'd heard the rumor her high school boyfriend had returned to his parents' boarded-up farmhouse. Apparently, he had built a makeshift runway on the deserted, muddy fields for an old cargo plane so he could fly emergency supplies into the flooded Midwest.

Max is back.

Each time the silent reminder popped into her head, she felt her heart plummet to her toes. Lord help her if she ran into him in town. What would she say? How would she react to him? Thankfully, he had kept pretty much to himself. Word was he had been gone most of the past week, anyway—which had made her rest a little easier. Not much, but a little.

With a tired sigh, she closed her eyes and pinched the bridge of her nose, trying in vain to rid herself of the dull ache in her head, as well as the picture of Max in her mind.

Max is back. And she couldn't do a blessed thing about it except wait and wonder if their two worlds would collide.

"Elizabeth?"

She raised her head as Steve Walford took a red bandanna out of his back pocket and wiped the sweat from his forehead. Furrowed eyebrows told her that his news wasn't going to be good. "Number-three pump is almost out."

"We managed to save this old building in two other floods, Steve," she pleaded. "Isn't there anything you can do this time?"

"Doesn't look good." Steve stashed the bandanna. "Without that third pump the basement will flood for sure. When it does, the oil furnace and water heater will go out. Those people you got living here better evacuate to the Red Cross shelter at the high school gym."

Elizabeth appreciated his help. Steve had a knack of showing up whenever a crisis arose. Perhaps she depended on him a little too much. She could handle just about anything that life had thrown at her, but it was still nice to have his advice, his friendship. In his mid-forties and divorced, Steve had made it quite clear that he was interested in Elizabeth, a good ten years younger. But she couldn't regard him with anything more than deep friendship.

She stood at the front steps with Steve and his cohort Tug Mazzey, another local business owner who was trying to help her save the old building from the rising river.

What they didn't know and what she couldn't tell them was that the seven women and their kids could not go to a crowded shelter where an ambitious news reporter might expose them on television. No one in town knew that the renovated McKenzie boarding house harbored women from the nearby Saint Louis area who had fled violent relationships.

"I'll find another pump," she said with more confidence than she felt.

Both men looked down at the groaning machine.

"You know it won't be that simple," Tug argued. "There's none left within hundreds of miles up and down these rivers. Everyone's fightin' the same fight you are, hon. And they're not getting the amount of volunteer help that they got before. You can't expect folks to give up their own pumps and risk losing their homes just so you can save this old building."

"It's not just a building I'm trying to save, Tug."

"We know," Steve answered solemnly. "We know."

Elizabeth looked out at the leaden skies and the slowly encroaching Mississippi. It had already laid claim to a parking lot across the street and was about to breach the four-foot embankment alongside the empty road. When it did, it would pass the watermark of previous floods. At least the traffic jam of sightseers was finally gone. The National Guard had positioned a barricade up the hill to keep away all but the property owners and designated volunteers working the pumps.

"Can you keep this thing running long enough for me to get a pump trucked down from Chicago?" she said.

"With bridges out, that'll take longer than usual. More rain's expected, too. Doubt you'll get anything through in time." Steve was the voice of reason, but Elizabeth couldn't give up. Not yet.

"Let me worry about time," she said. "Just tell me how much longer before the basement floods."

Tug stroked his double chin in contemplation. "If you had a good mechanic and the right parts—two days, tops."

"Are you saying you two can't fix it?"

"We've tried everything," Steve admitted. "My guess is you need somebody who knows engines like the back of his hand."

"Yeah," Tug added, eyeing Steve. "Somebody who could jerry-rig just about anything."

"Max Wilder." Elizabeth hadn't realized she'd spoken his name aloud until Steve brightened and Tug looked confused. She held her breath, regretting her slip of the tongue.

"Of course! Wildman!" Grinning, Steve shook his head, as if reliving a distant memory. Surely, he didn't know about her intimate relationship with Max. Or did he? she wondered. He turned to Tug, explaining that Wilder was a local hell-raiser quite a while back. "Worked as a mechanic after school. Damn good, too. That boy was a natural. Joined the military to become a pilot." He looked at Elizabeth. "Weren't you livin' here back then? Before you moved to Chicago?"

Elizabeth nodded numbly, remembering those days all too easily. When Max had left to become an air force pilot, he was supposed to have come back for her. But their lives had taken a different course. She'd heard a few years ago that he'd won a big state lottery. It was hard to believe that Wildman was now worth millions.

"Good thing you mentioned him." Steve interrupted her thoughts. "I'd forgotten he was back. Making himself pretty scarce with all those relief flights he's been running. Sure surprised to hear about it, too. Don't recall him being the white-hat type."

"Definitely not," murmured Elizabeth, trying to imagine Max as a Lone Ranger riding to the rescue. It was no good. Max was more suited to a black hat and dangerous smile. Unless he was paid a king's ransom, he was never known to do anything without personal benefit.

"Money changes people." Steve shrugged. "He can afford to

play hero. And I bet he'd jump at the chance to fix that old pump for you."

She doubted it. If he had even the faintest memory of his days in Alton, he wouldn't want to lay eyes on her again, let alone help her save the old boarding house.

Elizabeth spoke more for the men's benefit than her own. She knew the odds were against her, but..."Do you really think that pump could be made to last long enough to get a new one?"

"Wouldn't hurt to ask," Tug said.

"Looks like you don't have any other choice." Steve crossed his arms over his sweat-stained work shirt, looking at her optimistically.

"I better get cleaned up before I go begging for favors," answered Elizabeth as she glanced down at her own soiled jeans and T-shirt.

"Good luck," offered Tug.

"Thanks." She tried to rustle up a smile as she said goodbye. Walking to her car, she felt the butterflies in her stomach take flight.

Max was back.

And she needed him.

~

MAX LEFT HIS BOOTS in the mudroom of the farmhouse and walked into the kitchen, where he rummaged through his mom's old Harvester refrigerator for something to eat. The lack of a microwave whittled down his immediate choices to an apple and a beer. He chose the beer.

Leaving the aluminum cap on the yellow Formica next to the sink, he wandered through the dining room and stopped in the doorway to the living room. Familiar furniture sat right where it always had, most of it draped with faded floral sheets. Max had uncovered only the old man's brown recliner, the maple end table next to it and the television. He didn't need much else while he was living here. Except maybe some fresh air. The sky-high humidity had managed to seep into the closed-up room, suffocating him with the moist, musty smell of a dead house.

He swigged the ice-cold beer, welcoming the chill in his throat. Crossing the worn-out carpet, he rolled the chilled bottle over his forehead, wetting his skin. The pale green drapes were open, but dingy sheers hung in all four windows. He was lifting the sash of the last one when he spotted the mud-splattered sedan turning left into the driveway.

"Real-estate brokers," he muttered to himself, taking another pull on the longneck. Too tired to deal with another agent pressuring him to list the farm, he stepped aside to avoid being seen by the woman emerging from the car parked in the shade of a tree at the end of the concrete walk. With one finger, he drew back the sheer curtain a fraction of an inch to peer at her. Though her door blocked most of his view, he noticed white sandals and slender ankles. They looked sexy as hell, but he couldn't imagine what possessed a woman to wear strappy little sandals while driving around the muddiest roads on the map. Given any other circumstances, Max would've welcomed the opportunity to pursue an attractive woman. But the pretty package didn't change the fact that she was undoubtedly after a listing. Nobody but a real-estate agent would bother to drive clear out to the farm. And he was in no mood to be seduced into selling his folks' place.

Late-afternoon sunlight silhouetted the visitor. Something about her seemed familiar. A sense of unease settled in his gut. She paused at the opening in the white picket fence, where the gate hung open with morning glories twined around it. Her long skirt and white blouse made him think of old photographs in the family album that had been painted in soft pastels. Her dark blond hair was loosely pinned up off her shoulders. Her hands reached up and removed a pair of sunglasses.

"I'll be damned." His awestruck whisper hung in the heavy air.

She hesitated, then slid the glasses back into place and started toward the house. He ducked behind the drape.

Hearing light footsteps on the wooden porch steps, he glanced down at his socks. One big toe poked through a hole. The cuffs of his jeans were caked with dried mud. His light blue T-shirt had engine grease streaked across the front.

The broken doorbell emitted a pathetic, abbreviated *dink*. He peeled off one sock and let it drop to the floor, then hopped to the door as he yanked at the second sock. When Liza Jane pressed the button again, he balled up the holey sock and tossed it across the room toward the first one, but it fell short, landing on the lampshade.

Disgruntled with his poor shot, he pulled open the heavy oak door.

Elizabeth smiled brightly. Too brightly, she knew. But she couldn't stop herself, any more than she could stop the flutter of starlings that had taken flight in her stomach.

The years vanished as she gazed at Max standing behind the screen door with his black hair a little too long and those dark blue eyes staring right into her. She felt sixteen all over again. Her mouth dried up. Her thoughts scrambled. Worst of all, her body tensed with the same sexual electricity she had felt with the eighteen-year-old "Wildman" Wilder.

"Hi, Max." She dipped her head and removed her big sunglasses again. "It's me."

"I know."

She held her breath, waiting to see if he would slam the door on her. His narrowed eyes studied her from head to toe and back again. Then he said her name in a soft whisper that took her back to drive-in movies and haylofts. "Liza Jane..."

She nodded, afraid to trust her voice.

"You've changed," he said, shaking his head in disbelief.

"And I haven't been called Liza Jane in years."

"Is it *Elizabeth the Classical Actress*?" He remembered the way she had once rattled off her dream as if it was one long name.

"Just Elizabeth."

"You shortened it."

She smiled modestly. "We had great aspirations, didn't we? At least you attained yours—becoming a pilot."

Max felt a knife twist in his stomach when she mentioned aspirations. He had enlisted in the air force, expecting to go on to flight school while she majored in drama in college. But the summer after her high school graduation, she started talking marriage and babies. He thought they were both too damn young. Then one day he got her letter, telling him she had married Johnny and moved to Chicago. His folks never filled him in on any details, which was fine with him.

"How have you been?" she asked nervously.

"Not bad." Remaining in the doorway, he didn't bother to invite her into the empty house. She'd probably come to satisfy her curiosity about her ex-boyfriend. Once she realized that a few million bucks hadn't changed him from being a grease monkey, she would hightail it back home. Just as well. He didn't need her around here dredging up memories. "How about you? I was going to try and get into town to say hello when I had a chance."

It was a lie, but he couldn't exactly tell her that he'd been avoiding her like the plague.

"I guess you couldn't know—"

"About Johnny?"

"He died, Max. Two years ago."

"I heard," he admitted quietly. Sensing the sadness in her voice was like having a fist slam into his chest. Max hated the man for stealing Liza Jane, but he'd never thought the jerk would up and die on her. "I... uh, read about it in the Phoenix paper."

She shook her head, then glanced down at her feet, as if mustering up courage from beneath the peeling floorboards of the porch. When she looked up again, her full lips curved into a weak smile, but her eyes were bright with unshed tears. "Plane crash. Ironic, huh?"

She turned and gazed out at the horizon, hugging her arms as if a chill had somehow gripped her in the midst of the muggy heat. "You were the one who was the reckless kid playing daredevil pilot. You were the one I was afraid was going to die in a plane crash. After everything that has happened, I'm not too crazy about flying anymore. I can't imagine that you do it every day without any fear whatsoever."

Max was surprised by her confession. She still thought about him? She even worried about his flying? All this time he'd been wondering about her, wishing things had turned out differently, dreaming of her in his life. But he had assumed she'd forgotten all about him.

"I guess it is a bit ironic, at that." The old screen door squeaked as he stepped out onto the porch and stood behind her, watching the sky grow darker. He didn't know what to say about Johnny. Despite their close friendship, there had always been a childhood rivalry between the two of them. Johnny had always come in second to Max. Until Liza Jane. The true irony was that Johnny was gone and his widow was now standing here on the front porch with Max. His friend had lost out again.

"I'm sorry about Johnny," he offered honestly.

She pivoted around and looked up at him. A tear had run down the side of her cheek, leaving a glistening wet line. The last time he'd seen her cry was at the end of his Christmas leave all those years ago. She hadn't wanted him to go back to Germany without her. But this time she wasn't crying for him. She was crying for another man, the man she'd lost just two years ago.

"Thanks for coming by to say hi," he said, then nodded to the ominous sky. "It looks like a storm's blowing in. You better get on back."

She allowed herself a small chuckle. "Those were the same

words you used to say when I'd come by that old filling station where you worked."

"I recall you weren't much for listening to my advice... or your daddy's threats."

Back in those days, Max had been every father's worst nightmare—a hot-tempered eighteen-year-old whose nickname, Wildman, said it all. Max had paid no attention to the younger Liza Jane until the night he had another fight with his girlfriend. He was nursing his bruised ego and Liza Jane was too damn eager to console him. In hindsight, he never should have got that six-pack of Bud. After drinking a can, she changed from the chubby, freckle-faced sixteen-year-old into a hot, voluptuous seductress. Something in his gut had warned him she was a virgin, but she sure as hell didn't act like one. She was more than any hormone-driven teenage guy could imagine. He never meant for things to go as far as they did. That night was only the beginning. Right or wrong, he couldn't stop going back to her.

But there'd been something more between them, something other than great sex. He couldn't exactly name it or even admit to it. All he knew at the time was that he couldn't breathe without Liza Jane Brown. Liza Jane was his, and his only.

Or so he'd thought.

Right up until the day she'd married his best friend.

He yanked his thoughts back from the past and glared at her. "I hate to cut this short, but—"

"I need you, Max."

CHAPTER 2

*M*AX STARED AT HER for a long moment.

"Go home, Liza Jane." The spring on the screen door complained as he flung the door open and stepped into the house.

Elizabeth caught the edge of the wooden frame before the door banged shut. "I don't mean... That is, I came to ask for your help. To fix a water pump."

He slowly turned around. "Your house?"

"No. It's the—the McKenzie building." She silently swore at her tangled tongue. The brick boarding house had been in John's family for generations. Her marital connection was one more reminder of her betrayal, of the pain she had caused him. Sensing the escalating tension between them, she launched into a hasty explanation. "Steve Walford and Tug Mazzey have about given up trying to keep the water out of the basement. We all agreed you're the only one who could patch it up long enough for me to find a new one."

He folded his arms across his chest. "Let me get this straight. . . You're trying to get *me* to save a dilapidated old building that belonged to *Johnny?* Now ain't that sweet. No thanks."

Max left her standing there, strode toward the stairs and took them two at a time. She could hardly be angry at his predictable reaction. But she couldn't give up without a fight. It had always been that way with Max and her. She knew if she wheedled and cajoled, she could talk him into anything. Well, not exactly. Not marriage and babies. A flicker of regret darkened her thoughts before she mentally shoved it aside.

"Where are you going?" she asked through the screen door. "I'm not finished—"

"I'm going to take a shower," he called back over his shoulder, before disappearing around the corner.

Elizabeth walked inside, determined to wait in his living room until he came back downstairs. She glanced around at the shrouded furniture. Memories washed over her of Mr. Wilder molded into his favorite chair, watching TV. Harry could be a tough old man when it came to disciplining Max, but he had quite a soft side when it came to his wife, Martha. In their household, Elizabeth had known a special kind of love—strong and sturdy. Not like her own home, where cozy appearances masked the private lives of parents who displayed no affection toward each other or their only child. How many nights had she dreamed of marrying into Max's family, of one day making this house her home? She had imagined the children that would fill the rooms with laughter and love.

But it never happened.

She knew seeing Max again would be rough. But she was willing to risk it. She didn't anticipate other ghosts of their past coming back to haunt her, as well. Tears welled in her eyes at what could have been, what should have been. Realizing the direction of her thoughts, she silently reminded herself of John and their two children. If things had gone differently, she would not have Brodie or Annie in her life now. It was time to stop the if-onlys. The past was behind her. She had to keep her mind on the road ahead.

Determined to solve her immediate problem with the water pump, she dashed up the stairs and knocked on the door of the bathroom "Max!" she hollered over the sound of the shower.

When Max didn't respond, she knocked louder. "I'm not leaving until you give me a chance to explain."

"Call me on the phone. Tomorrow."

"This can't wait until tomorrow."

"I'm too tired, Liza Jane."

"It won't take that long, I swear."

"Ha!"

"Please, Max..."

When the water was shut off, Elizabeth heard raindrops slapping the window at the end of the hall darkened by the arrival of the storm. A long, low rumble vibrated through the house.

"Max?"

"I heard you, dammit." As the bathroom door opened, a roll of thunder barreled across the fields, making the walls around them reverberate with the sound.

Max was very nearly naked. Water dripped from his jet-black hair and ran in rivulets down the sprinkling of black hair on his chest. The familiar tattoo on his upper arm drew her attention, reminding her of the careless whim of two young lovers. He had the Tasmanian Devil with his nickname under it. She had planned to have "Wildman" etched above her left breast, over her heart, but he talked her out of it which secretly bothered her. They were going to be together forever. Why would he object to his name on her permanently? Unless he didn't feel the same way about her. Disappointed, he had balked at her suggestion of inking her name on his bicep, she accepted his choice for her— the tiny rosebud on her right butt cheek, discreetly hidden for his eyes only. At the time, she wondered why he wanted her to hide the symbol of their love from the world. Now, she was relieved it was hidden. Not even her kids knew about it. But it would always be a reminder of Max.

His hand clasped a blue bath towel draped around his hips. The evidence of his arousal was obvious. Elizabeth swallowed hard and looked away, startled by her own flood of desire.

"What did you expect when you started that begging routine on me again, Liza Jane? Or did you forget what it used to do to me?"

"I *did* forget, Max." She had indeed forgotten their provocative adolescent game. She put her palms up and backed away, her lower lip tucked between her teeth, trying to mask a sheepish grin. "I swear I didn't mean for you... that is—"

She bumped into the opposite wall and a lightning flash made her jump.

Max closed the small space between them. He braced his free hand on the faded, cabbage rose wallpaper, blocking her escape. When he dropped his mouth to hers, she let out a muffled squeak of surprise. But as his tongue slipped between her lips, he heard her soft moan, just before a deafening clap of thunder charged the air.

He wanted her.

Leftover love had nothing to do with it. Sex with Liza Jane had always been downright incredible. Wild. Explosive. He wanted her one last time, to remind her what it was like between them, to make her regret leaving him. He wanted her to say she'd made a mistake, that she should have waited for him instead of marrying Johnny.

Feeling the light pressure of her hands against his chest, he lifted his head and gazed into green eyes full of confusion.

She whispered, "We shouldn't."

"I know."

Her breathing was as ragged as his. It was wrong to extract his perverse idea of revenge, and he knew it. Yet he kissed her again, deeper and harder. The taste of her made him hunger for more. Her heart pounded against his chest. He knew he should stop, but he couldn't. With Liza Jane, he never could stop the fire once it started to blaze out of control.

"Max... don't..." Even as she spoke, her hands crept under his arms to his back. Her fingers dug into his wet skin. He moved his hand from the wall and cupped her face. Deep inside his chest, he felt his bitterness melt away. Holding her and touching her again had taken away all the pain.

"Leave," he pleaded, no longer willing to punish her for the past. "Leave while you still can."

"I—I can't."

"You already did once before," he reminded her, trying to force her to make the right decision for both of them. Then, God help him, he nuzzled the soft indention between her shoulder and neck. Her skin was damp from perspiration, tasted of salt and smelled of her own familiar scent. His mind flashed images of her lying beneath him. Tanned body. Bikini lines. Milky-white breasts.

His kisses moved up to the sensitive spot behind her ear. The scent of her perfume made him harder still.

The towel around his waist dropped to the floor as she curled one leg around his, sliding her heel up the back of his calf. Somehow, somewhere along the way, she had slipped out of her sandals. He didn't know when, and right now, he didn't care.

A bright flash accompanied the loud crack of a tree struck by lightning. Max watched the storm raging in her green eyes.

"Don't hate me," she breathed, "for what I did to you."

"I don't. Not anymore." How could he tell her that his hatred had dissolved the moment she touched him? How could he explain that he needed her in more ways than he could ever say, more than his body could convey?

His lips brushed across hers once, twice, until she took control. Her teeth nibbled his lip, then her tongue darted into his mouth. Her hands skimmed down his back and cupped his buttocks, pulling him closer as the storm unleashed its fury.

Amidst the lightning and the thunder, he wanted nothing more than to thrust himself inside her and blast through the dark clouds of their past, flying higher, beyond the memory of teenage ecstasy in the back seat of a Dodge.

But something stopped him. A force he couldn't understand held him back.

As he buried his face in her neck, he held her tightly. He knew it could have been just like their first time—hungry, hot and wild. And, just like their first time, he would have felt guilty as hell afterward. They weren't kids groping and pawing and rushing before anyone caught them.

He wanted her back more than ever. But not this way.

"I'm sorry, Liza Jane."

Elizabeth felt a certain despair as he stepped away from her. The warmth and intimacy of being held in his arms brought back the sweeter memories of their tempestuous relationship. In her starry-eyed adolescence, she believed that great sex was equal to unconditional love. For a moment, she had fallen for it again. How could she have let her guard down so easily?

She let the wall support her, certain her legs would give way if she tried to stand on her own. As thunder rolled outside, she thought she would never hear that driving force of nature without recalling this unabashed longing for Max to drive himself deep inside her. Despite her humiliation, she couldn't lie to herself. Her body ached for fulfillment. In those few minutes, she had felt more alive than she had in two years.

In the last several years, an inner voice mocked.

No, that's not true!

She had loved John with all her heart. He had been a good man, a good husband. Then why did she throw herself at Max within moments of seeing him again? What if he'd shown up three years ago, when John was still alive? Would this have happened then?

Closing her eyes, she bowed her head. "I'm sorry, too. I shouldn't have driven out here."

"No, you needed me," he said softly, tilting her chin up with the crook of his finger.

"Not like this." She turned her head aside, unable to look at him. She stepped around him and went into the bathroom. Before closing the door, she hesitated, her back to him. "I didn't intend for this to happen."

"Neither did I, kid," Max muttered as he scooped up the towel and headed for his bedroom. "Neither did I."

~

WHEN MAX HEARD LIZA JANE coming out of the bathroom several minutes later, he had already dressed and wandered downstairs. Although the intense humid heat had let up somewhat due to the rain, the sticky warmth still smothered him. His cotton work shirt was already damp from perspiration. His beer was warm and flat, but he didn't give a damn. He took a drink anyway, grimaced and slugged down another mouthful.

He watched her descend the stairs. She had found her sandals and fixed the mess he'd made of her hair. Putting down his bottle of beer, he strode toward the bottom step.

"Can I get you something to drink?" he asked, knowing he didn't have anything to offer but a glass of water, knowing he should just let her go out the front door without another word.

She shook her head, her gaze only lifting high enough to touch the first button on his shirt. "I'm fine."

Liza Jane was under his skin already, and he couldn't do a damn thing about it but stand there asking dumb questions.

"I'll follow you into town and take a look at that pump you were talking about. It's the least I can do."

Her head jerked up. "For turning me down?" She paused on the second step, her narrowed eyes level with his. "You did us both a big favor, Max. Don't feel you're obligated to make amends for it."

Her clipped words matched her stiff steps down the last two stairs. He grabbed her arm as she passed by and gently pulled her around to face him.

"What I did up there..." He searched for the right words, but he had never been one to explain himself. He just did what he chose, and if people didn't understand him, that was their problem. But it was different now with Liza Jane. "I turned you down *because* I want you."

Confusion shadowed her green eyes.

"Just let me fix the water pump so I won't feel so damn guilty for hurting your feelings."

She sighed heavily. "Believe it or not, you that you did not hurt my feelings. If anything, I'm feeling foolish for letting myself get carried away. It felt good to be held in a man's arms again, to be kissed again, to feel something again. But the last thing I want or need is to go back to the past. In fact, I should thank you for keeping me from making a big mistake."

He experienced a flash of jealousy over being a substitute for Johnny. "Are you finished?"

"No." Elizabeth looked down to his thumb rubbing the sleeve of her blouse, his warmth penetrating the cotton material. Extracting her arm from his grasp, she looked him straight in the eyes, daring him to find a trace of emotion for him still left in her heart. "I wouldn't have come here if it wasn't my last chance to save the McKenzie building. I still need that water pump fixed—whether or not I like your reason for helping me."

"I'll get my boots on."

"I'll be in my car." Leaving him standing at the bottom of the stairs, she walked outside, silently berating herself for going upstairs, for forgetting how she used to goad him, for letting him kiss her senseless.

She dashed through the rain and scrambled into the driver's

seat without getting too wet. The raw force of the thunderstorm had swept through, leaving the soil saturated beyond capacity. The land didn't need any more water.

And she didn't need any more of Max Wilder.

Waiting for him to bring his own car around to follow her into town, she stared at the drops that fell from the branches of the tree and landed on her windshield. The life she had built with John would not be washed away as if it had never existed. John had cherished her. Not Max.

The vivid memory of her first night with Max always stirred up feelings of self-recrimination, twisting her insides until she had to press her fist to her gut to stop the pain. She had been a love-struck kid of sixteen, willing to do anything to get Max. Elizabeth remembered the shameless flirtation of a naive girl who did not know enough to understand she was in over her head until it was too late. She soothed his bruised ego and mistook sex for love. Only when he'd called her by his girlfriend's name did Liza Jane realize her mistake. She was a substitute for the girl he really wanted. She couldn't blame him for taking advantage of her. Not after she threw herself at him.

More than her innocence had been lost that night. Sending Max back to his first lover would have been the best solution to regaining her self-respect. But she loved "Wildman" too much to let go.

Elizabeth wondered what would have happened to her relationship with Max if John hadn't been there for her, if she hadn't married him. Even though she did not have the wildly passionate sex with John, he made her feel safe and secure.

Since his death, she had tried to maintain her self-sufficiency, to maintain the feeling of security she had with John. Now Max was a threat to that security. But trying to stop him was like trying to hold back the raging river with a few sandbags.

A black, late-model pickup pulled out from behind the farmhouse with Max behind the wheel. She reached for the keys she had left in the ignition and gave them a twist. Nothing happened.

"Come on," she coaxed, giving it another try. Silence. "I don't need this. Not now."

During the last several weeks of mounting tension over the water level and levee breaks, not once had she broken into tears or a tirade. Too many people depended upon her—her two children, John's mother, the women and children at the shelter. Seeing Max, however, did not help matters. The uncooperative car was an insignificant problem, yet it magnified her frustration.

She tried again without any luck. "No..." After months of being strong, she cursed the sobs that finally broke through. Damn the car. Damn the rain.

"And damn you, John, for dying on me." Cleansing tears poured out the frustration and fear she had held back for ages.

Her door flew open. "What's the prob—" Max leaned down beside her. "Liza Jane? What's wrong?"

"It—it won't start," she answered between gulps of air, knowing how foolish it must seem to cry over a dead battery. She covered her face with her hands. When he gently took her wrist, she let him pull her out of the car. Under the protective boughs of the old oak tree, she leaned into him as his arms wrapped around her and held her tight.

It felt so soothing when he rubbed her back. When his lips pressed against the top of her head, the warmth of his breath seeped through her skull. Yet she continued to cry.

She didn't want to want him as much as she did.

CHAPTER 3

*H*OLDING HER CLOSE, Max squeezed his eyes shut, wishing there was someone around to kick his butt for doing this to her. It was his fault she was crying. Even though she'd betrayed him, he still felt overwhelmed with guilt. Through his own stupidity, he'd made her feel rejected, pushed aside. He couldn't blame her for hating him. She should be slugging his chest and calling him a bastard, not clinging to him and crying as if she blamed herself.

After a couple of minutes, he escorted her to the cab of his Ford truck, then went back to her car for her purse. As he tossed it onto the seat next to his hat, she thanked him.

"No need." He closed the door and started the engine, looking over at her. Strands of damp hair clung to her neck and the side her face. Her wet white blouse had become almost transparent, revealing a white lace bra and the outline of her nipples.

Mentally cursing the immediate tightening in his jeans, he trained his eyes on the instrument panel, shoved the gearshift into reverse and backed the truck away from her car.

On the road, he searched for something to say to take his

mind off their little mistake upstairs. "You've changed your hair —it's a lot darker."

She sniffed, taking a tissue from her purse. "No more bottles of peroxide."

"I thought it was your natural color."

"Surprise," she said in a flat tone.

She was skinnier now, too. While she had slimmed down considerably during their three years together, she had dropped so much more weight she appeared fragile.

He figured a compliment might cheer her up. "You're... a lot thinner."

With a strained smile, she shifted uncomfortably. "Thanks," she said, then looked out her window. Obviously, he figured wrong. He only succeeded in making her self-conscious.

Max turned on the radio and fiddled with the dial until he found a Garth Brooks song. She glanced at the dial, then at his black cowboy hat lying on the seat.

"What happened to Metallica?" she asked.

"Guess I've changed a little, too." He tried to relax, but the awkward conversation only reminded him of the days when they had been able to talk nonstop—especially Liza Jane. She could fill in the gaps with just about any topic under the sun. He'd teased her that sex was his way of getting a few minutes of peace and quiet, though they'd both managed to make a lot of noise even then. Damn, they'd been great together.

"The truck smells new," she observed.

"Picked it up at Roberts Motors the day after I got back. Still haven't figured how I'm going to get it back to Arizona..."

"I heard you won a lottery a few years ago." She picked up his hat and smoothed the black felt brim. Max remembered when she had sat next to him and slid that same hand up and down his thigh. "Must be nice."

Better than nice, he thought, recalling the sexual undercurrent of their past together. Then he answered her comment about the money. "It has its perks. But I wish my dad would've let me spend some of it on him before he died last year."

"I'm sorry about Harry. Martha, too, even though she's been gone for some time."

"Yeah... well, thanks." As another shower pelted the truck, they barreled down the raised highway, which was a good fifteen feet above a flooded field. "How're your folks?"

"Moved to Florida five years ago. I haven't seen them since John's funeral, when I moved back to Alton."

"Why?"

"Ask them," she said, putting the hat back on the seat cushion.

Like him, Liza Jane was an only child. And, like him, her teenage years hadn't been easy ones. But that's where the similarities ended. His parents had been farmers. Hers were displaced city people who never quite settled into the rural life. They'd expected her to marry a notch or two above the level of a guy like Max Wilder.

He remembered her old man threatening to kill Max if his little girl got in trouble. What Mr. Brown didn't know was that sweet little Liza Jane had a hidden wild streak as wide as the Ol' Miss itself. That was one of the things Max loved about her. But there had been something desperate and lonely in her eyes when she looked at him. Something she'd wanted from him that he couldn't give. Not until it was too late, anyway. All these years later, he finally understood why she'd wanted a family of her own —she was searching for a love that was missing in her own home, with her own parents. He thought of her with Johnny and their two kids, then realized she'd gotten what she'd wanted. Max could see that now.

"I didn't mean to dig up ill feelings about your folks," he offered apologetically. "I guess I was pretty lucky with mine. Took me years to appreciate them, though. I sure was no Boy Scout."

"Your parents thought the sun rose and set on you. Your

mother used to say you were just sowing wild oats. She was certain you'd settle down sooner or later."

"Too late for them to see it, though."

"Is that why you're here, Max? Are you somehow trying to make up for your less-than-shining past?"

"Naw... That thought never crossed my mind. I can't change the past, no matter how much I might want to." He paused, realizing the blatant implication of his words, then quickly went on. "I've made a lot of mistakes in my life. But I think I've learned some lessons, grown up a bit and maybe even matured. I thought it was time to let my lucky lottery money do some good for somebody other than just me."

"Money changes people."

"Occasionally for the better." Uncomfortable talking about himself, he changed the subject. "I was wondering what brought *you* back to Alton."

Max took his attention off the road long enough to glance at her. She looked over, saw him watching her and quickly averted her gaze.

"John's mother," she finally answered. "She invited me to live with her."

"Couldn't you make it on your own?"

"That's not why I came home, Max. Bernice was distraught. I can't imagine what it's like to lose a child."

Max heard the tenderness in her voice. Liza Jane had always held a soft spot in her heart for kids. She loved babies. Wanted a dozen of them. Then it dawned on him that he'd almost made love to her earlier without a single thought of protection. If he hadn't stopped, certainly she would've said something about birth control. Wouldn't she?

"Max?"

"Hmm?"

"You've gotten awfully quiet all of a sudden."

"I was thinkin'."

After a moment of silence, she prompted, "About...?"

The accelerated rhythm of his heart kept time with the windshield wipers slapping back and forth. "About what happened upstairs."

"Can we forget about that?" she pleaded, closing her eyes and tilting her head against the back window of the truck, her face flushed with embarrassment. Returning his attention back to the road Max wished there was something he could say to make her realize he hadn't meant to humiliate her.

"I have one last thing to say on the subject, then I won't bring it up again." He pressed on without giving her a chance to object. "I said I wanted you, but I don't think you believe me." He paused, waiting for her response. When none came, he interpreted her silence as agreement. "It wasn't that I didn't want you, Liza Jane. I just wasn't prepared... that is, I didn't plan—"

"Neither did I."

He held up his hand. "That's exactly my point. You could have gotten pregnant."

"Not likely," she murmured, though he doubted she intended to be heard.

"Are you on birth control?"

"I don't sleep around."

"I'm not implying any such thing. I was just asking."

"Why would I use birth control with John gone?"

"Then why are you so sure?"

"Medical reasons, okay?"

Max suddenly thought of all the possibilities and settled on the worst one of all. The roar of the water in the wheel wells was drowned out by the rush of blood to his brain.

He had to force the question out of his mouth. "Are you sick?"

Elizabeth watched his knuckles tighten around the steering wheel, his face turn pale.

"It's not cancer," she said, touched by the expression of relief that immediately washed over his rugged features. He didn't need to know that her female functions had stopped operating the past six months. "If I could conceive—which I can't—I wouldn't put myself at risk. I haven't forgotten how you feel about children. I certainly heard it often enough—you did not want to be a father."

"I told you I wasn't *ready* to be a father. There's a hell of a lot of difference. And I wasn't ready to be married, either. But you couldn't wait. You had to be Mrs. Somebody, so you ran off with Johnny."

"That's not how it happened," she said softly.

"Refresh my memory then, Liza Jane. That Christmas I was home on leave, we spent half our time parked on some remote back road. When I got back to Germany, I thought long and hard about us. Just when I'd decided to come back in the summer with an engagement ring, I ended up getting your polite little letter about you and Johnny."

Elizabeth winced inwardly at the cold rendition of his side of the story. From his perspective, she was the ultimate spoiled brat who had stabbed him in the back.

The elevation of the road gradually dropped. Max cussed loudly and downshifted to a crawl as the truck entered a pool of standing water that had seeped through sandbags. A handful of drenched volunteers were filling more canvas sacks and stacking them higher. The scene sobered her. While those people worked in the rain to save their fields, she and Max were comfortably dry in the shelter of the truck cab, hashing out past history, opening old wounds. She had nearly forgotten that their verbal sparring matches had been as passionate as the sex. But she didn't have the energy to keep up with Max anymore.

She stared straight ahead. "Yes, Max. That's how it was," she lied with quiet bitterness. Receiving no rebuttal from him, she sensed her sudden acquiescence had stunned him into silence. They rode the rest of the way into Alton without further word.

PULLING UP TO ONE of the barricades downtown, Max rolled down his window, letting in the steady drizzle as the guard in fatigues and a green rain poncho walked up to the truck. He looked too young to be out of high school, let alone in uniform. When the young man politely requested some identification of residency and explanation for entering the restricted area, Liza Jane moved the cowboy hat to the dashboard and slid across the seat, offering her driver's license. She leaned against Max in order to talk through his window. The warmth of her breasts against his arm stoked the smoldering embers left over from the fire they'd started at the house. As usual with Liza Jane, all it took was the slightest touch—innocent or not—to set him off.

Repressing the urge to shift uncomfortably in his seat, he caught sight of the kid ogling Liza Jane's cleavage with more than just puppy-dog eyes. Max also didn't like the way she encouraged the guard with her bright smile.

He turned his head and whispered a grumpy command in her ear. "Say goodbye, dammit."

As the guard removed the yellow plastic ribbon and let them pass, Liza Jane asked, "What was that all about?"

"I'm dead tired," Max complained, wondering if he would have had the energy to make love to Liza Jane at the farmhouse. "I want to get this machine of yours fixed and get home so I can sleep for a week."

He drove a block, turned left and descended the hill toward the McKenzie building on the bottom corner. The lower street was almost under water. At the intersection, a long, wood plank walkway with safety rails accessed the Alton Queen Riverboat, a floating casino that remained open, though permanently docked until after the floods. Nothing bigger than a canoe was allowed to run on the river. The saturated levees and fragile sandbags could not withstand the destructive wakes of larger watercraft.

Max parked the pickup against the curb alongside the brick building, put on his hat and opened the truck door. He started around the hood toward the passenger door, but Elizabeth grabbed her purse and slid out before he reached her. She hurried past him, stopping abruptly at the wide stream running down the gutter.

Without a word, Max gently swept her off her feet and waded through in his cowboy boots.

"Damn-fool sandals," he muttered, walking through the water.

"My tennis shoes were wet from traipsing around the basement." She refused to admit that she had secretly wanted to impress him.

After he deposited her on the other side, she murmured her appreciation before she continued down the sidewalk. Max acted as if his courtesy was standard treatment for any woman who was nuts enough to wear sandals. Perhaps that was exactly why it was so unnerving to have noticed the flexing muscles of his arms where she had placed her hands for balance, or to feel the lingering warmth of his fingers on her rib cage beneath the swell of her breasts.

At the corner, Elizabeth dashed up the front steps, waving to Tug Mazzey, who was standing under an umbrella by a pump near the other end of the building. She entered the front door, followed closely by Max. In the foyer, Steve Walford was talking with Bernice McKenzie, John's mother.

The slim, graying older woman turned from her conversation and welcomed Elizabeth with a maternal smile. When her gaze dropped to the damp blouse and long skirt, her eyes expressed concern. "Why on earth are you wearing such good clothes in this rain? Where are your jeans? And your boots? Land sakes, child, you're soaked."

"Not quite." Elizabeth chuckled, accustomed to the good-natured mothering. "I was almost dry before we had to run through a few sprinkles to get in here. Five more minutes in this heat and I'll be wishing I was wet again."

When Bernice spotted Max, the twinkle in her pale blue eyes

vanished. An expression of stunned surprise, then a kind and gentle smile crept over her face.

"Mom... Steve," Elizabeth began, stepping to one side. "You two remember Max Wilder, don't you?"

Steve immediately leaned forward with a quick handshake. "Good to see you again, Max. Congratulations, by the way—nine million, wasn't it?"

"Six-point-nine," Max corrected with a self-conscious grin.

Steve whistled appreciatively. "One big chunk or yearly payments?"

"One big chunk," Max answered without the swaggering pride Elizabeth would have expected from him in his younger days.

"I heard you bought yourself a place in Arizona and one helluva an antique plane. Sure is great of you to come back to help the homefolks out."

"Glad to do it."

Bernice said to Max, "I've been wondering if you'd ever get around to coming to see me since you got back."

There was a moment's hesitation as the two studied each other. Then Max awkwardly extended his hand in greeting. "Hello, Mrs. McKenzie."

"You've never called me Mrs. McKenzie, so don't go starting it now." Ignoring his gesture, she opened her arms in welcome.

Max stepped into her embrace, giving her a tight squeeze before he released her. Elizabeth felt her chest tighten at the emotional reunion of her husband's mother and his best friend.

"I'm sorry about Johnny," he offered.

"Thank you." Bernice paused, gazing at him with a question in her eyes. "I didn't know how to let you know. I wish you could've come to the funeral."

"I..." He cleared his throat, then simply said, "Me, too."

She patted his arm. "I'm so glad you finally had a minute to stop by."

"Actually, I dragged Max into town to fix the water pump," Elizabeth said.

"She didn't need to drag me," he protested.

Bernice glanced from one to the other, then settled her gaze on Elizabeth. "You weren't grocery shopping?"

Steve spoke up. "After Tug and I did all we could with that old pump, Elizabeth went out to ask if Wilder might be able to help. I thought sure I told you, ma'am. My apologies."

Mrs. McKenzie's expression of concern evaporated, replaced by a casual gesture of dismissal. "I'm acting like a fretful old mother hen. With this flood and all, I tend to worry too much about which bridge or levee might go next." She turned to Elizabeth. "I guess I was a bit surprised to hear you'd gone clear out to the Wilders' farm by yourself."

Elizabeth felt the tension seep from her muscles, relieved to learn her mother-in-law had been concerned about the long drive, not the reunion with Max. And yet she was unable to alleviate her guilty feelings.

It was only a kiss, Elizabeth reasoned with herself. But she knew all too well that she had been willing to take it far beyond that seductive kiss.

Mentally closing the door on that particular memory, she quickly offered to take Max outside so he could get started on the pump.

Steve stepped forward. "I'll do it, Elizabeth. No sense in you getting wet a second time today. I'd feel bad if you were sick in bed with a cold when I plan to take you out to dinner tomorrow night."

Caught between the possessiveness in her friend's eyes and Max's curious observation, she was in no position to correct any false assumptions by either of them. "I've always done my share of work, just like everyone else around here," she argued. "Damp clothes haven't stopped me so far. And they're not about to now. Come on, Max."

As she turned to leave, he rested his palm on her shoulder. "He's right, Liza Jane. Stay inside. Besides, I could use a good, strong cup of coffee."

Elizabeth didn't appreciate his firm command any more than she liked his open display of concern. It wasn't like Max—the old Max, anyway. There was a time she'd longed for any public acknowledgment of his feelings. But that time had passed. Ignoring her own belated sense of pleasure, she decided against any further protest. Clearly, both men preferred to handle the situation without her help.

Hiding her disappointment, she sighed heavily and waved at the door with a flip of her hand. "Go for it, gentlemen. Us womenfolk will just stoke the fire and keep the hearth warm for y'all."

Her humorous attempt at sarcasm brought a chuckle from Steve. But Max only gave her a cocky grin and a wink that made her heart hammer.

CHAPTER 4

*A*s Max and Steve departed, Elizabeth followed Bernice down the hallway to the kitchen, knowing her mother-in-law would not pry, yet sensing her unspoken questions about Max. She was relieved to find two of the women boarders washing the lunch dishes, while three of the youngest children played underfoot and a baby slept soundly in an infant seat placed safely out of harm's way on the floor.

When a shy toddler rubbed one eye and whined for his mama, Elizabeth lifted him into her arms and took a seat at the table, reassuring him that his mother would be back soon. She knew little Danny couldn't understand that each mommy took turns filling sandbags in the community. Unlike the other kids, he was untouched by a violent past. Born six months after his mother had arrived at the boarding house, the dark-haired little boy took to Elizabeth, who welcomed the opportunity to hold him close. Sometimes she felt he gave her more comfort than she gave him.

Allowing her to rock him to sleep, Danny was soon snoring softly while the four adults talked. Bernice prepared a fresh pot of coffee, then joined them at the table. Several minutes passed before the status of the basement was brought up. Elizabeth assured them that everything possible was being done and that none of them would be stranded without a place to live. Clearly relieved, the two boarders excused themselves to check on the older children in an upstairs playroom.

"I'll bring Danny up in a little while," Elizabeth offered, savoring the maternal contentment of having his warm little body snuggled against her. After the women left, she lowered her face to his silky, soft brown hair, closing her eyes as she inhaled his sweet scent of baby sweat and powder. A familiar longing emerged from deep inside her, a longing that had been locked away in a dark corner and forgotten.

You want his baby, said her inner voice.

A long time ago I did, she silently answered as Danny nuzzled against the softness of her breast.

What if he hadn't stopped and you had gotten pregnant?

No chance.

Nothing is impossible. Once is all it takes. You already know.

"Why are you frowning?" Bernice interrupted her thoughts, crossing to the cupboard.

Elizabeth wasn't about to reveal the pointless argument going on in her head. But she did have a question on her mind. "I didn't realize you knew Max was back."

"When Sam Roberts came over to man the pumps, he told me Max picked up a fancy new truck at his dealership that morning." Bernice took out four heavy ceramic mugs. "Figured that boy would get around to finding you one way or another."

"He didn't find me."

"No, but that doesn't really matter now, does it?"

Bernice brought two filled mugs to the table. She sat down across from Elizabeth and lifted her mug halfway to her mouth, a soft light of understanding in her eyes.

"It's been two years," she gently reminded her. "I couldn't exactly hold it against you if you took up with him again."

Elizabeth masked her surprise, thankful she had not been

holding the hot coffee when she heard the startling comment. "I appreciate your generous outlook about my social life, Bernice. But I'm not ready to *take up* with anyone." *Especially Max Wilder.*

"I know you loved Johnny—"

"I *did* love him."

"Yes... and I'm glad. You turned out to be a real fine wife for him. He couldn't have asked for better."

She slid one slender hand toward her daughter-in-law. Elizabeth silently extended her palm until their fingers touched. There was a special friendship between them that transcended their mutual connection to John. Elizabeth could speak her mind on anything without judgment from Bernice.

But Elizabeth refused the invitation to discuss her husband's childhood friend and rival, Max Wilder. She refused to acknowledge any feelings she might still have for Max—let alone any possible future with the man—despite their passionate kiss. She had simply been caught up in the nostalgia of a teenage romance, nothing more.

Bernice lightly squeezed Elizabeth's hand, then released it and settled back in her chair. "Thirty-six is too young to be wasting away."

"I'm not wasting away. I love my work here, helping the women and their children." She stroked Danny's dark hair affectionately.

"You can't help others if you don't see to your own needs first." Her mother-in-law sipped her coffee before she spoke again. "You can't starve yourself this way."

"I'm not starving myself," Elizabeth argued softly. "I just don't seem to have much of an appetite anymore."

"You haven't been eating properly for far too long now. If Johnny were alive..."

"He'd talk some sense into me, I know."

"You two were good for each other," Bernice stated plainly,

giving Elizabeth's hand a light squeeze, then returning to her coffee. "Mind what I said about taking care of yourself."

"I'll try." She looked down at the baby in her arms. Bernice had reason to be concerned. Elizabeth had undergone a doctor's exam to determine the cause of her weight loss and menstrual problems, only to learn it was stress. Between John's death and the floods, she had more than her share of stress. She certainly didn't need to add to it with Max coming back into her life.

Realizing Danny had slumped into an uncomfortable position, she shifted his slumbering body so that she cradled him in her arms.

At that moment, Max came through the door. "Steve told me he'll take a rain check on the coffee."

His booming voice startled Elizabeth as well as Danny.

Max stopped, his eyes riveted on the baby.

Then, holding his black cowboy hat in his hands, he crossed over to the long table. When his dark gaze rose to meet hers, Elizabeth knew exactly what he was thinking—that the child was hers. She was about to tell him otherwise, but Danny began to fuss, claiming her attention. When she caressed the little boy's chubby cheek, her fingers trembled. As she rocked, Danny popped his thumb into his mouth and settled back to sleep.

Delighted in her small triumph, Elizabeth looked up at Bernice, who glanced at the shaking hand, then directly into her daughter-in-law's eyes, cocking one eyebrow in an all-too-knowing gaze. The older woman rose to her feet and turned to Max. "Have a seat while I get your coffee."

After hanging his hat on the back of an empty chair, he dropped into the chair next to Liza Jane. "Is it yours?"

Elizabeth chuckled lightly. "He's not an *it* and he's not mine. This is Danny. I'm babysitting for a little while." She didn't feel he needed to know the real purpose of the boarding house.

She continued to rock Danny, wondering if Max overheard the conversation about John. When she met his gaze, she couldn't read anything but the fatigue in his dark blue eyes that watched her intently, reminding her of a few fleeting moments in his arms.

"Steve and Tug offered to pick up some bubble gum and shoe-strings for me to fix the pump," he said quietly, with good-natured sarcasm. "They'll be back in a half hour."

"Can it really be repaired?" Bernice asked, concern written across her soft features.

"Ought to be able to keep running awhile longer. You've got to get a new one in here as soon as possible."

As Bernice fretted about finding a replacement pump at this late stage of the floods, Liza Jane promised she would locate one even if she had to personally travel from coast to coast.

When Bernice placed the mug in front of Max, he thanked her. Ignoring the sugar and non-dairy creamer in the center of the table, he sipped the black coffee, desperately needing a jolt of caffeine, but craving a shot of whiskey. He didn't know which had him more rattled—mistakenly assuming the baby was Liza Jane's or accidentally eavesdropping on the two women. He couldn't quite figure out why he was relieved to learn Elizabeth wasn't the little boy's mother. But he bristled over Bernice's comment that John and Liza Jane had been good for each other—not when she had belonged with him.

Still, he couldn't help noticing that the marriage must not have been too bad.

The tenderness in her voice when she spoke of Johnny taunted him with a possibility he didn't want to face—that she genuinely loved John McKenzie.

The sound of someone approaching in the hallway brought Max back out of his reverie.

Bernice perked up. "Steve must be back."

"That was quick," Max mumbled, then took a gulp from his cup and put it down, reluctant to head back outside.

But Steve Walford didn't appear in the doorway. Instead, a tall young man in a wet T-shirt and cutoff jeans smiled at them.

"Hi, Mom. Hi, Grandma."

Max shot a questioning look at Liza Jane, who avoided his gaze. He knew she had a son, but this one was a helluva lot older than he'd expected.

Liza Jane spoke softly over the baby's head. "I thought you were helping Jessica and her folks."

"She doesn't need me anymore, so I figured I'd check if the basement's doin' okay."

A nearly grown-up son. Max felt as though he'd taken a fist in the chest. Liza Jane might not be able to get pregnant now, but she had managed just fine about sixteen years ago. And the boy didn't look one bit like Johnny.

"We're all right so far. Come here and meet an old friend of your dad's and mine... Max Wilder. He's going to fix the pump. Max, this is my son, Brodie."

Max pushed back his chair, stood and extended his hand. "Glad to meet you, Brodie."

"Yeah. Same here." The boy responded with limited enthusiasm and a brief handshake. Max recognized the familiar green eyes, the same dark shade of jade that belonged to Liza Jane.

"Excuse me for staring, but I didn't realize your mother and dad had a son as big as you. You're taller than your daddy was at your age, which would be... sixteen, I'd guess?"

"Fifteen," Liza Jane volunteered too quickly. Max felt a twinge of regret as his suspicions evaporated. If Brodie was fifteen, then the boy couldn't possibly be his.

"But I'll be sixteen pretty soon," Brodie interjected. "I've got a birthday coming up the first of September. That's only a little over a month away."

"Really?" Max glanced at Liza Jane. Her eyes pleaded with him. "I suppose you're ready for some wheels."

"I got my eye on a '73 Chevy truck I want to fix up," he mumbled, dropping his gaze to the floor.

"Grease monkey, huh? Did your dad teach you?" Max knew that Johnny hated working with engines.

The kid glanced up and shrugged. "Naw... Just comes naturally, I guess."

"Like me." Max sensed the tension in Liza Jane as she stroked the baby's back. "You ought to talk to your mom about taking more interest in her car. It broke down in my driveway this afternoon. It's still sitting there."

"Oh no, Elizabeth, not again," Bernice exclaimed, reminding Max that the three of them were not the only ones in the room.

"It's just a dead battery," she said defensively. "I think."

"You see?" Max gave a wry smile.

"You see nothing," she countered. "That car has been working fine. Sort of. Until lately. Anyway, I'll get someone to drive Brodie and me out there tomorrow with a new battery."

"I'm going right by the parts store on my way home. I'll take you back after I work on the pump."

~

THE STEADY RAIN WAS STILL FALLING as Max and Liza Jane hurried to his parked truck. His legs felt like lead. Although he had gulped down two cups of coffee before finishing the pump, he didn't feel the slightest boost in energy. The backs of his eyelids were gritty, as if someone had used his eye sockets for sandbags.

"Give me your keys," she requested urgently, her shoulders hunched against the rain. "I don't dare let you get behind the wheel." When he balked, she added in frustration, "No macho crap, Wilder. Real men can ride shotgun with a woman driver without having their masculinity questioned."

Her crack brought a crooked smile to his lips. He unlocked the driver's-side door, then relinquished the keys to her before he went around to the other side. By the time he reached his door, she had unlocked it with the power button. He took off his hat, dropping it on the seat, and slid in next to it.

Without looking at him, she started the engine and pulled away from the curb as a rowdy rockabilly tune blared through the speaker by his ear. Despite the distraction of the country song, Max couldn't get his mind off the almost-sixteen-year-old boy. While they moved along the slick, wet streets of Alton, Liza Jane concentrated on her driving, unaware of his watching her. At least she acted unaware.

The auto parts store was closed. Standing at the locked glass doors set under a wide overhang, they read a handwritten sign explaining the owner had left to sandbag his house. The home phone number was posted "in case of emergency," which was ironic, considering the entire population was in a state of emergency.

Liza Jane said wearily, "Even if we call him, you're too tired to wait for him to drive over here and open the store, let alone install that battery once we get to your place."

"You've got a point," he admitted reluctantly.

"If you drop me off at the house, will you be able to drive yourself home?"

"I'll manage." He didn't know how, but he'd do it.

They were back on the road when he began to nod off during a lulling ballad about lost love.

"It's raining pretty hard again. You could sleep at my place," Liza Jane offered, hastily adding, "Only for an hour or so... at least until it lets up."

Max kept his eyes closed, but smiled. "I got a better idea. You could drive me home, and we'll come back for the battery in the morning."

"Spend the night?"

"Yep."

"With you?"

"With me." He resisted the urge to open his eyes to see whether her expression showed reluctance or temptation.

"But this afternoon—"

"I made a mistake."

"So did I."

"Yeah. . . Like marrying Johnny instead of me."

Again, he refused to look at her, choosing to wait for her usual return fire. But it didn't happen. Instead, she continued the conversation as if she hadn't heard him.

"Even if I wanted to spend the night with you—which I don't —there would be too many questions if I didn't come home tonight."

"Bernice?"

"Brodie... and Annie, my nine-year-old."

"Does *she* look like John? Because Brodie sure as hell doesn't." Max rolled his head to one side and watched her.

"He's not your son, Max."

"He was born the first of September."

"I know when he was born. I was there."

"And I was home on leave the last two weeks of December. That's just about nine months."

She drove in silence, almost running through a four-way stop in a residential section of Alton.

"And don't tell me you were sleeping with John at the same time," Max continued. "I won't buy it for a second."

"Thank you for your vote of confidence. You're right—I wasn't going back and forth between you."

"Then you admit—"

"I know how it looks," she said, taking the corner too fast. "But Brodie came six weeks early."

"Bull."

She yanked the steering wheel and careened into the gravel driveway of the two-story house. When she pulled to a stop between the screened porch and the tall evergreen shrubs along the property line of Bernice's house, Max was glad for seat belts and new tires.

She shoved the gearshift into Park, pulled on the emergency brake and swung around to face him. "It was hard enough on Brodie to lose his dad. I won't have him spending the rest of his life wondering if the man he'd worshiped might not have been his father."

"So you'd rather have him worship a dead father instead of me —his *real* father."

"I should slap you for that."

"Who's he going to blame when he finds out you kept the truth about us from him?"

Elizabeth killed the engine, realizing that Max wasn't going to leave until they'd cleared the air. She stared out at the rain slanting across the narrow driveway. "If it wasn't for you, I never would've had him."

Max threw up his hands. "Hey, this is one mistake you can't blame on me. If you'd have told me you were pregnant, I would've married you."

"Oh... right." She rolled her eyes in dramatic disbelief. "I forgot how badly you wanted to make me your wife."

"I'd already decided to propose to you on my next leave."

"And when did you come to this decision? Before or after you'd heard that your first girlfriend had gotten married?"

"Debbie had nothing to do with it."

Elizabeth shook her head. "Deb had *everything* to do with us. You never would have noticed me if she hadn't left you. Do you remember when you got her wedding announcement? I do! Right after you went back to Germany. After we'd spent the holidays together. You wrote to me in January, telling me that she must have enjoyed rubbing salt in an old wound."

Max looked stunned. "I told you about that?"

"I guess you didn't think it would hurt me that you were still agonizing about Deb. Even after being with me for three years, you still weren't over her. But her marriage ruined your chances of getting her back."

"I know I wouldn't have written anything like that, because it's not true." Max tossed his hat on the dash and slid across the seat. "Is this why you married John, even though you were carrying my baby? Because you thought I didn't love you?"

Elizabeth closed her eyes and tilted her head back. "When I got your letter, I showed it to John that night. I needed answers. I wanted to know if you would have gone back to her if she'd asked. I thought he could help me figure out if I was wasting my time with dreams of marrying you. He knew you. He was your friend."

"Some friend."

She opened her eyes and looked at him. "He was my friend, too—which was why he hated seeing me torn up over you. He was angry at you for telling me about Deb, about your bitterness over her wedding announcement."

"Did he also think my letter implied that I'd wanted Deb back?" Max draped his right arm over the steering wheel as the pounding rain echoed inside the cab.

"No, not from reading your letter. But he did say that you took it pretty hard for months after she left you." Elizabeth allowed herself a small, bitter laugh. "He didn't know you were sleeping with me during all those months."

"I didn't think you'd want me to tell him."

"How kind."

"Did *you* tell him?"

"I told him everything—including that you called me Debbie when you made love to me the first time."

Max winced. "I guess I was a real son of a bitch."

She smiled sadly. "John's words exactly. He said I deserved better than you."

"And he suggested somebody like him?"

"Not exactly. He told me that if I'd have been his girl, he would've treated me like a queen."

"Smooth line," he muttered.

"It wasn't a line, Max. Maybe it would've been for you. But John wasn't like you when it came to girls."

"Obviously not. You chose him over me."

"No, it wasn't like that. It was... an accident."

CHAPTER 5

$\mathcal{M}$AX EYED HER SUSPICIOUSLY. "What do you mean an accident?"

"I thought you didn't love me, that you never loved me. John was there for me. His mom was out of town. We were alone. We never intended anything to happen."

"Brodie?"

She nodded.

"Did it ever occur to you that you might have already been pregnant that night?"

"You always made sure we were protected."

"Condoms are known to fail."

"I started my period the day after you left."

"Oh."

"I never meant to sleep with John. We weren't thinking, especially about birth control. Things just got carried away."

"Considering what almost happened this afternoon, I guess I'm in no position to judge." Max lowered his arm and laid his palm on her flat stomach. "These last few hours I spent thinking Brodie was my son, I was surprised by the strange feelings inside me. I wish we could go back and start over again and have our own kids together."

Elizabeth felt the heat of his hand penetrate into her womb, moving her far more than an intimate caress. "You said yourself, we can't go back."

"But we can start over."

"There isn't going to be another baby, Max."

"I know you said you can't get pregnant, but you already did. Twice. So whatever is wrong, I can get you the best medical help that money can buy."

"Even if I could conceive, it's too late for us."

"I've wasted too many years regretting losing you. I should've married you years ago. But I didn't, and I'm sorry. I'm sorry for making you so miserable that you ended up in the arms of another man. Everything has changed now."

"Yes, it has changed. We're different people than we were then. Despite my behavior this afternoon, I'm not Liza Jane anymore." She wrapped her fingers around his hand and moved it away, his tenderness too much to bear.

"You can't deny that the sparks are still there."

"All right, I won't deny it. I wanted the fireworks again. But you didn't. Obviously the sparks weren't there for you."

"You're wrong."

"Am I? Then tell me why you put on the brakes."

"I've asked myself that same question, but I couldn't come up with any answers until now. I was afraid of letting my guard down, of letting you bring back all the feelings I've carried around for you all these years. I didn't want to be hurt again."

"Neither do I. I'm glad one of us had the instinct to know we were about to make another big mistake. Can't you hear what you're saying, Max? When we look into each other's eyes, all we see is the pain we've caused. We're no good together." She grasped the door handle to get out of the truck.

"Liza Jane, wait." When she hesitated, he reached up and cradled her cheek. "I'm no saint when it comes to women. But nothing ever compared to what we had together. Not even close."

"Sex isn't everything in a relationship, Max."

"Who told you that? Johnny? It figures."

"Stop it." She shoved his hand aside. "I *loved* John. Or is your ego too big to accept I loved somebody other than you? A steamy kiss shared in your upstairs hall doesn't change the fact that I had a happy marriage with John."

"*Had.* He's gone, Liza Jane."

"You will be, too, when this flood-relief whim of yours is over."

"Whim?" His dark eyes narrowed. "That's what you think this is? A lousy whim?"

"Yes, as a matter of fact, I do." She felt a twinge of guilt for her admission. The words, the feelings seemed to tumble out on their own accord. "Do you want to know what your problem is, Max?"

"I have a feeling you're going to tell me."

"You have more money now than most people will ever see in their entire lifetime, enough money to buy anything you want. But that's still not enough for you, because you always want what you can't have. You haven't changed. You're still a kid with a box of toys, wishing for the new train in the store window."

"Looks that way, doesn't it?"

"When you had your chance with me, you wanted Debbie. Now you want me because you know you can't have me. One night of marathon sex and you'd get me out of your system and fly off back to Arizona."

"Not a chance." He leaned closer, a glint of mischief in his midnight-blue eyes. "A week, maybe."

She leaned back. "Two nights, tops."

He kissed her softly, breaking away again before she could retreat. "Three nights. Final offer. But I need at least a week of sleep before we start."

48

She couldn't hold back the smile as she shook her head. "We're not starting anything. Anywhere. Anytime."

"That's what you think." He kissed the tip of her nose and dropped his cowboy hat on her head, then reached past her to open her door. As she hopped out of the cab, he slid over and followed behind her in a mad dash through the rain.

On the porch, Elizabeth removed the hat and shook off the water before handing it to him. "Thank you."

"You're welcome."

She led him into her house where he left the hat, brim up, on a chair by the door. He trailed behind her as she walked through the living room, calling for her daughter. A car horn honked in the street out front.

"Hi, Mom!" A whirlwind of motion bounded down the stairs and rounded the newel post. Dropping her sleeping bag and backpack, Annie barreled into her, arms held wide for a hug. After a quick squeeze, she turned toward the door. "Bye, Mom!"

"Hold up there, young lady. Why are you leaving so early?"

Annie pulled up short and spun around, her blue eyes pleading. "Mandy called and said her mom wanted to pick me up before supper. I left you a note on the kitchen table. Can I go now?"

"Yes, but first show your manners and say hello to Mr. Wilder. He's a high school friend of your father's and mine."

Annie blinked, as if she hadn't seen him standing in the living room until that moment. Her face lit up immediately. "Hi, Mr. Wilder."

"Hi, Annie." Max extended his hand. The girl blushed pink, accepting his gentle handshake. "Nice to meet you."

"Same here." She gave him a coy smile while her gaze remained transfixed on his face. Elizabeth could hardly blame her for staring. Max could dazzle females of all ages. A second honk sounded outside, drawing Annie's attention, however reluctantly. She looked down at her hand, still grasping Max's, then sheepishly withdrew it. "I, uh, I gotta go."

"Have a good time, sugar," murmured Elizabeth, watching her child heft her gear and dart out of the house. "See you tomorrow."

"Uh-huh. Bye!" The door slammed shut, rattling the rafters.

Elizabeth didn't mind. She was grateful that her daughter could still go on being a kid no matter what disasters went on around them.

"Cute kid. Looks a hell of a lot like Johnny."

Smiling, Elizabeth nodded. "I know. She was her daddy's little girl in every way."

"So... we're alone?" Max asked, suggestion in his voice.

Caught off guard by the sudden change in topic, she couldn't bring herself to look at him. She didn't want to be drawn to him like a fascinated child to a flooding river. Despite a deceptively calm surface, swift-moving water swept away everything in its path. Max was no different. He would sweep through her life and leave her heart battered and broken after he was gone. One way or another, she knew she would survive the ravaging Mississippi, but she wasn't so sure she could survive Max.

"Brodie and Bernice should be home in about half an hour."

"We can do a lot in a half hour."

She turned to find him lounging against the doorjamb, his hands stuffed into his back pockets, his damp hair as black as flint. Lord, he looked inviting. The electricity between them made her blood pulse in places inside her only he could reach.

"You're too tired, remember?" A sweet ache in her thighs reminded her of the exquisite pleasure she was passing up. "Maybe you'd better use my bed."

"Good idea." He extended his hand. "Come with me."

She stepped forward, determined not to give in to him.

"I'll show you where my room is. Then I'm leaving you there.

Alone." Elizabeth led him back through the living room and up the stairs.

As they entered the large master bedroom overlooking the street, she announced, "Excuse me while I grab my robe. I need to get out of these wet clothes and take a shower."

She ducked into the walk-in closet and came out with her white terry bathrobe, somewhat amused to see Max once again leaning in the doorway.

"You can't even stand up without support." She paused at his side, shoulder-to-shoulder. "Go to bed, Max."

He lazily hooked an arm around her waist. "I wouldn't give up so easily if I wasn't about to fall over."

"Exactly why I offered my bed," she said dryly, retreating down the hall.

"You're awful cocky."

"Sweet dreams, Wildman."

Elizabeth closed the door of the bathroom, undressed and stepped into the small tub, closing the frosted-glass door behind her. As she stood under the shower spray, her body throbbed with the awareness of Max, only a short distance away. It would be just like him to feign exhaustion to put her off guard, then show up behind her and make love to her under the warm water. She felt the tingling anticipation creep into her breasts, drawing her nipples taut, then spreading downward like hot milk.

Why did Max have this effect on her?

She vigorously scrubbed her skin, trying to scour away the old memory of his hands intimately exploring her. But it was futile. Afterward, she slipped into the long robe, then combed her hair while she padded barefoot down the hall. As she passed her bedroom, she paused at the open doorway and looked in.

Max lay splayed out across her floral bedspread. He had stripped off all but his jeans. Intending to close the door and leave him sleeping, she reached for the doorknob. But even in his sleep, he had a magnetic pull on her. Leaving the door ajar, she crossed the soft peach carpet and stood between the bed and her bentwood rocker.

He snored lightly, his bare chest rising up and down with his gentle breathing. Her gaze rose to the pillow cradling his head of thick black hair. His dark lashes lay against his tanned skin. She noticed a tiny scar on the bridge of his nose. Leaning closer, she saw the slightest indention and wondered if he had broken it at one time.

He began to move and she jumped back, ready to bolt from the room. As he rolled to his side, she realized he was too tired to wake up. She also needed a nap, but she didn't dare lie down on the bed next to him. With his instincts, he would assume he was dreaming and make love to her in his sleep.

If he asked, you could tell him he imagined it all.

Elizabeth plopped down in the rocker, refusing to believe she was actually contemplating something so deceptive. She could never stoop so low.

Then why haven't you left?

This was the challenge she needed. She wanted to believe she could sit here without being drawn to him. She had to prove to herself that she had the power to withstand his attraction.

The soft patter of rain on the window soothed her raw desire for the man lying on her bed. The slow, rhythmic creak of the wooden rocker calmed her frenzied need to push aside all logic and join him. She smiled to herself as her eyelids drifted shut.

See, Elizabeth? Max Wilder does not have a magic hold over you.

MAX DIDN'T WANT to wake up yet, not while he was dreaming of Liza Jane. But a cold shower could solve his problem and he'd get right back to sleep. Opening his eyes, he realized he was not in his old bedroom at the farmhouse. His gaze fell upon Liza Jane dozing in the rocker next to the bed, her head lolling to one side, a comb in her relaxed hand.

After returning from the bathroom, he sat on the edge of the bed. When she shifted uncomfortably, her robe gaped open. He felt himself harden at the sight of her small breast and the dusky rose circle around her nipple.

Swearing silently, he stood and pulled back the bedspread and sheets, then lifted Liza Jane from the rocker and lowered her to the mattress. Her sash dropped to the sheet and her robe fell open completely. He stifled a groan.

He wanted to make love to her, no doubt about it. Yet she looked so fragile, so breakable. She was beautiful, but waif thin. It almost scared him to think of his heavy body on top of her. He'd probably break one of her ribs. She wasn't the full-breasted Liza Jane with thighs that had tightened around him in a grip that drove him wild.

Max recalled Bernice's concern earlier in the kitchen and Liza Jane's response—*I'm not starving myself. I just don't seem to have much of an appetite anymore.*

"What's happened to you, Liza Jane?" he whispered, tracing a finger delicately along her rib cage. His heart swelled with an overwhelming need to take care of her. His chest tightened at the thought that losing Johnny had done this to her. She had once been a rose in full bloom, and now she was withering away. She must've really loved him, Max realized, envy tearing at his insides.

He wanted to be loved like that.

Somewhere deep inside him, he must have known that he was still in love with her. But he couldn't admit to it. Until now. He wanted a second chance. He needed her. And whether she knew it or not, she needed him to bring her back to life again, to make her blossom like a rose again. Max drew the coverlet over her slender body and tucked it under her thin arms, then leaned over and brushed his lips across hers.

"I'm going to do whatever it takes to win you back." His voice was barely loud enough to hear. "I won't lose you again."

He watched her sleep as he put on his shirt and boots, then quietly slipped out of her room and went downstairs. He retrieved his hat from the chair, smiling at the memory of it on Liza Jane's head. She sure looked cute. He was still grinning as he walked out the front door and nearly collided with Brodie. The startled teenager carried a rain-dampened sack of groceries in one arm, while holding the screen door open with his free hand. He glanced past Max into the empty living room.

"Where's my mom?"

"Upstairs." Max hitched a thumb over his shoulder. "She was pretty tired. She's taking a nap."

The boy didn't appear convinced. Max didn't mind if the suspicion in Brodie's eyes was directed at him, but he didn't want Liza Jane to lose her son's respect. Trying to act as if it was perfectly natural for him to be slipping out of her house as she lay asleep in bed, he gave the teenager a warning look.

"Don't go jumping to the wrong conclusion about me and Liza Jane—"

"Quit calling her Liza Jane." Brodie put the paper sack next to the door and faced Max with clenched fists. "While you're at it, quit coming around here. That's if you know what's good for you."

Even if the hackneyed threat sounded too much like a Hollywood western, Max knew better than to laugh at the stiff-faced delivery. The kid was half a twitch from taking a swing at him.

"I'm real sorry if you got the wrong impression," Max drawled, nixing the impulse to put a reassuring hand on Brodie's shoulder. "But the honest truth of the matter is that there's nothing going on between your mother and me."

Silence stretched between them as the boy weighed Max's words. Suspicious eyes showed uncertainty, then narrowed again.

"Liar."

Brodie turned and ran down the wooden steps and around the side of the house. Max was about to follow but stopped when he saw Bernice walking through the light drizzle of rain from her car parked on the street. His truck had prevented her from pulling into the driveway. As she mounted the steps with an armful of groceries and an umbrella, Max glanced at the corner of the house, then turned back to her to explain the confrontation with her grandson.

"I can't let him go off without straightening him out about Liza Jane."

"Leave him be." Bernice handed Max the sack, then shook the water off her umbrella. "If you haven't been up to your old tricks, I doubt it's from lack of trying."

Her frank remark hit a little bit too close, but not exactly dead-center. "Once a Wildman, always a Wildman—is that it?"

"Still got that chip on your shoulder as big as a city block."

"I've whittled it down somewhat over the years."

"I hope so, because what I'm going to say to you might not sit too well." She took the groceries from him and put them next to the sack that Brodie had deposited near the door. Turning to face him, she folded her arms across her chest. "John told me all about you and Elizabeth."

CHAPTER 6

Silent string of curses ripped through Max's mind. A few years ago, he might have slammed his fist into the porch post after hearing that Mrs. Mac knew about Liza Jane's none-too-perfect past with him. But he kept himself in check.

Bernice seemed to let her news sink into his exhausted brain cells before she spoke again. "When he came to me for some honest advice, he didn't hold back a single detail. By the time the two of them found out about the baby, I had no doubts about the fatherhood of that child. But I had plenty of doubt about that marriage."

"Liza Jane says she loved Johnny," Max offered with some bitterness.

"I know that girl tried hard to be a devoted wife. Land sakes, how it hurt me for the longest time watching those two together. As polite as two foreigners who didn't speak the same language. But they stuck it out, both of them. By the time Annie came along, you'd have thought their marriage was made in heaven."

The news hit Max like a dull slug to the gut. True as it seemed to be, he'd never get used to the idea of her loving anyone else but him.

"So she was better off without me, after all." His caustic murmur was meant more for himself than for her ears.

"She never had a day's doubt that John wanted anybody but her. You would've been a different story altogether. She never would've felt good enough to match up to that old girlfriend of yours. Sad to say, she never felt good enough for John, either. She was indebted to him for doing right by her for the sake of their baby."

"Is that what you think?"

"Put your hackles down," admonished Bernice. "Elizabeth never had a debt to pay as far as I'm concerned. She's been a good wife, a wonderful mother and a sweet daughter-in-law. I'm probably the only one who knows how much she's punished herself for the mistakes she made as a kid. How many of us wouldn't like a second chance to do over some of the things we did in our younger days?"

Max thought of the letter he'd written from Germany and anything else he'd done that led Liza Jane to believe he had wanted Deb instead of her.

Bernice paused and gazed at him, her jaw set. "If nothing else, you kids have some things to settle. One way or another, Elizabeth has to get on with her life. I'm worried about her."

"Are you saying I'm not good enough for her?"

"You could be the worst medicine for her right now."

"So you're siding with Brodie?"

"I'm not siding with anyone. I can't blame my grandson for being protective of his mother. I don't doubt for a minute that he's heard of the reputation behind your nickname, especially now that you're home again."

"I've changed."

"So has Elizabeth. She's not the same girl you knew in high school."

Max thought about the scene in his own upstairs hallway. That woman during the thunderstorm wasn't this stranger, Elizabeth. For a few brief moments, Liza Jane had come back to him.

Come back to *life*, from the looks of it. Clammed up somewhere inside that prim-and-proper widow was a woman who wanted to let her hair down and be that same high school girl again. He was sure of it.

His heart ached at a memory of Liza Jane standing on top of a grassy hill, knee-deep in wildflowers. Her upturned face basked in the warmth of the summer sun, her arms spread wide as if she welcomed the whole world. He'd made love to her right then and there on top of that hill. In the middle of sweet-smelling wildflowers. In broad daylight on that hot summer afternoon.

If only he could reach back and bring that memory forward, hold it in his hand like a photograph. He would show it to Liza Jane and remind her of the person who had been full of joy, of excitement, of enthusiasm for life itself. He had loved that most about her.

If only there was a way to find some small piece of Liza Jane inside Elizabeth. If only...

"Looks like the rain's stopped," Bernice said.

"I better get home." Max levered himself away from the porch railing and headed toward the wooden steps. Pausing, he slowly turned back, to see the older woman watching him

"Forget something?" she asked.

"I *did* show up for Johnny's funeral. But when I saw Liza Jane... Max glanced down at the toes of his boots, shaking his head. "I watched from a safe distance at the cemetery. After everybody left I paid my respects at his grave. I wanted you to know."

"Thank you, Maxwell."

"You're welcome, ma'am."

"I wouldn't mind if you called me *Mom* again."

His throat constricted. With a grateful smile, he touched the brim of his hat and walked to his truck, welcoming the cool, wet drops from the dark sky.

~

ELIZABETH SLEPT THROUGH DINNER and awoke the next morning in a groggy state of frustration caused by a dream of Max. Her body had been tricked into believing that the pictures in her mind had been real. Too real, she thought, agonizingly aware of the bittersweet ache of sexual desire.

As she stretched languidly beneath the covers, the cool sheets shifted over her bare breasts. The realization of her nearly naked state slowly dawned on her. Her arms were in the sleeves of her open robe. She vaguely remembered falling asleep in the rocker. How had she ended up in bed? When had Max left? Maybe the dream had been real.

No, she refused to believe it.

A vivid image of wild lovemaking flashed through her head. She pressed her palms to her eye sockets and groaned. Wasn't it bad enough the man had popped back—however briefly—into her life? Did he have to invade her sleep as well?

With more effort than she cared to admit, she steered her thoughts away from erotic memories. Yet over and over again, during her shower and while dressing, she found her mind wandering back to the realistic dream, which still made her legs feel weak. Each time, she forced herself to forget about Max. Contemplating the ramifications of getting romantically involved with him brought up one word: *Disaster.*

And she thought the flooding Mississippi was her biggest worry.

Elizabeth went down for breakfast, slowing her steps as she approached the kitchen doorway. A feeling of dread settled into the pit of her stomach. Once again she wondered what time Max had left yesterday. Had he left before Bernice and Brodie came home?

She squared her shoulders when she spotted Bernice sitting at the kitchen table, a folded newspaper lying next to her plate. Pencil in hand, she looked up from the daily crossword puzzle, peering over the rim of her reading glasses. Her expression was a silent inquiry of concern, not condemnation.

Elizabeth sensed tension in the room that might have something to do with Max, but she wasn't eager to bring up the subject.

The two women exchanged the usual pleasant "Good morning" while Bernice took her dish to the sink.

"There's a double helping of eggs left in the frying pan. I thought you'd be starving after missing dinner last night."

"I'm sorry about sleeping through supper. I only meant to take a short nap." Elizabeth was uninterested in a heavy meal but took a healthy portion anyway. She would at least try to keep the promise she'd made to Bernice about eating better. "I guess I was pretty tired. I slept like a rock."

"It's high time you got some decent rest," the older woman scolded gently. "But you need more than a good night's sleep, young lady. I wish you could take a real vacation this summer. Get away from this place. You'll come back with your batteries charged and feeling like your old self again."

"While everyone else is battling this flood? They are tired, too. I'm not jumping ship now. I'm needed here." She took a fork from the drawer and sat down with her plate in front of her. The food smelled good, but not enough to make her dig in right away. She reached for a pink paper napkin from the container in the center of the table.

"If you collapse from exhaustion you won't be much good to anybody, especially to your own two kids. They need you, dear."

Unfolding the napkin and smoothing it across her lap, Elizabeth listened to the soft admonition from her mother-in-law, who rarely interfered with the upbringing of her grandchildren. Elizabeth's earlier sense of dread returned.

"Do you mean both kids? Or are you talking about one in particular?"

"For the moment, I'm talking about Brodie. He and Max met up last night. On the front porch. I'm afraid it didn't sit too well with Brodie. He got the wrong idea."

Elizabeth closed her eyes with a mortified groan, then looked at Bernice. "Where is he now?"

"He's already up and gone."

"Gone?"

"Now, now, he hasn't run away. He went over to the Meredith place to work on their levee."

Even though her initial panic ebbed, Elizabeth was still worried. "Maybe I should drive over there—"

"I've already had a long talk with him, last night after Max left. The boy is still hurting pretty bad. He's worried about you hooking up with Wilder."

"I hope you told him I'm not *hooking up* with anyone."

"In a manner of speaking, yes. I managed to calm him down some. But he could use a heart-to-heart with you later on. Let him know he's still the man around the house."

"I'll do that."

"I've got to scoot if I'm going to get all my work done at the shelter and run some errands. Do you need a ride?"

"Yes. The auto parts store was closed yesterday." Elizabeth absently poked her fork into the eggs. "I'll wait for Brodie to help me fix my car later this afternoon, when he gets back."

"What about Max?"

She shook her head, pausing before taking a bite of food. "I'm not asking him for any more favors."

"I wasn't thinking about him fixing the car. I was wondering how Brodie might feel about going out to the Wilder place."

"Oh..." The fluffy eggs in her mouth turned into tasteless

rubber, and she swallowed with difficulty. Yet again, her thoughts were filled with the man who had turned her quiet and well-ordered life upside down in less than one day.

Why, Max? Why did you have to come back to Alton now? Why couldn't you have stayed away forever?

~

MAX FELT GREAT.

Radio blaring, he sped toward town in his new pickup, tapping his fingers to a sassy Martina McBride song. There was nothing like a good night's sleep to put a fresh perspective on life. Not to mention a little wheeling and dealing to make things go his way. With a couple of phone calls to the right people, he had located a Chicago company that would have a water pump available the first of next week. He could jimmy the one at the boarding house to last that long. Or so he hoped, anyway.

After making arrangements to pick up the new pump on Monday, he reserved a suite at the Four Seasons for the weekend. Then he made a call to Mrs. Mac. With a little sweet-talk, he convinced her to help him out—for Elizabeth's sake.

As he entered the old brick building, he removed his hat and found Bernice in a small office off the foyer. She was surrounded by piles of paperwork. "Where's Liza Jane?"

"Out at the pumps."

"I appreciate your help in this."

"Don't thank me until she agrees to this scheme of yours."

"With you on my side, how can I lose?" He swung the door open and gestured for her to step ahead of him.

She shook her head but gave him a big smile as she passed him. He dropped his hat back on his head as she led him past Tug, sitting in a lawn chair by the front stoop. The river had crept closer to the boarding house while the pump kept chugging away in a futile effort to pipe water back over the sandbags.

When they rounded the corner, Max spotted Liza Jane in blue jeans and boots near the back of the lot. Slender hands stuffed into her back pockets, she stared down at the number-two pump. The rain had let up—for the moment, at least—so she was wearing only a denim shirt, the tails tied at her waist. She looked even better than she had the day before, if that was possible.

Strange how he couldn't look at her without feeling light-headed. His heartbeat drummed in his ears. His chest tightened. If he didn't know any better, he might wonder if he was having a heart attack.

"Somebody's here to see you, Elizabeth," Bernice called out.

Max watched Liza Jane turn around. For a split second, her eyes widened with surprise and he caught another glimpse of the girl he used to know. But it lasted for only an instant before she turned back into the cool, sophisticated Elizabeth. Still, he noticed the nervous way she tucked a wisp of hair into the smoothed-back hairstyle. He was relieved he wasn't the only one feeling skittish.

"Hope you don't mind my dropping by unannounced."

"Not at all." She gave a nonchalant flip of her hand. Too nonchalant, Max thought. Liza Jane couldn't quite carry off the air of indifference. "Nice to see you again."

"It's good seeing you, too." His gaze flicked to her toes and back in an appreciative once-over.

Bernice folded her forearms across her waist. "Elizabeth has been on the phone all morning trying to track down a pump in one of the nearby towns."

"No luck, I take it."

Liza Jane appeared reluctant to admit the truth. "No."

"Then pack your bags. I found one in Chicago. We can fly there tonight and pick it up on Monday."

Elizabeth shook her head. "I can't just take off with you for two whole days." *And nights.* Try as she might, there was no denying that a tiny part of her thrilled at the idea. But she wasn't about to heed the ancient call of the wild. Not where Max Wilder was concerned. She couldn't afford to put herself into any tempting situation with Wildman. "I have too many responsibilities to leave right now."

"No problem." He gave a not-too-innocent look on Bernice. "I'm sure there's nothing Mrs. Mac can't handle by herself for a few days. Right... Mom?"

"Of course I can manage." Bernice turned to her daughter-in-law. "Elizabeth, you know how I've been saying that you need some time away. This is the perfect opportunity. I'll hold down the fort while you're gone."

Glancing between the co-conspirators, Elizabeth repeated, "I can't possibly go today." She wasn't a lovesick girl anymore. There were Brodie and Annie to think about now, not this reckless pilot from her past.

Disappointment was written in his dark eyes, but he shrugged indifferently. "Suit yourself. I suppose I don't *really* need you to tag along."

Bernice protested, "You're not traipsing off to Chicago alone to buy a new pump for us. One of us should go with you to purchase it. After all, you're doing enough by flying up there to get it. So if Elizabeth won't go, then I will."

He grinned. "Fine by me. Be ready in two hours. There's another storm front headed this way. I want to be out of here before it hits this evening."

Elizabeth threw up her hands. "Hold on a minute here. Bernice, you're not going with him for two days, are you?"

"One of us needs to."

"Hey!" Max acted mildly offended. "You don't have to make it sound so terrible."

Bernice touched his arm. "I'm sorry, Maxwell. I meant that one of us should go along to write the check and fill out the paperwork."

Elizabeth propped her fists on her hips. "But I don't see why you insist on flying up there today. Why not Sunday? Or Monday morning?"

"Do you want me to risk being grounded by that storm coming through?" he asked, agitation twitching at his jaw. "There's no telling how long it'd be before I could fly out of here. That dying pump might not even last till Monday. Are you willing to take that chance?"

"No." Understanding his predicament with the weather, she felt a little foolish for assuming he had an ulterior motive for the extended weekend. She glanced at Bernice, feeling even more guilty for forcing her mother-in-law to take the trip. "There's no need for Bernice to fly to Chicago."

"I'll be perfectly fine!" the older woman remarked staunchly.

"I'm sure you will." Elizabeth was aware of Bernice's apprehension about airplanes, especially since John's death. Not that she herself was happy with the idea of flying, either. But they needed that water pump. With a sigh of resignation, she looked at her mother-in-law. "I suppose I could use a couple days away from this place."

"It's settled then," announced Bernice, a little too pleased with herself. She wasn't the only one. Max stood with his arms crossed on his chest, a lopsided smile of approval on his handsome face. As her stomach did another flip-flop, Elizabeth couldn't help sensing she'd been duped.

"Two hours?" she asked Max.

He checked his watch. "One hour and fifty-five minutes."

She lost her train of thought when he looked at her. His dark gaze took her breath away with recollections of the past. Familiarity. Intimacy. If one glance could do this to her, how in the world was she going to manage during the weekend ahead? She gave herself a mental shake and turned to Bernice.

"I'll need a ride home."

Max said, "I'll take you."

"No," Elizabeth quickly answered, then added, "thank you just the same. You've done enough already without interrupting your last-minute errands to drive clear back to my house." The more he did for her, the more indebted she felt toward him. She didn't like it very much. But desperate times didn't give her any choice. She did, however, have this one small opportunity to keep him at a safe distance, even if it was for a little while. "I need to go over a few things with Bernice before I leave, anyway. So I think it'd be best if she and I went in her car. Otherwise, I won't be ready on time."

He conceded with a nod. "All right. I'll see you soon."

~

BERNICE PARKED HER BUICK in the driveway just long enough to drop off Elizabeth. They had taken a few minutes to stop at Mandy's house so Elizabeth could say goodbye to Annie. The engine now idled as the two women gave each other a quick hug.

A look of concern flickered across Bernice's face.

"Good luck, sweetheart."

"I know there's no point asking you not to worry. But I promise to call as soon as we land in Chicago." Her words didn't seem to do much to reassure her mother- in-law.

"Don't you mind me," she said with a shake of her head. "And don't put a thought toward the kids or the shelter. Just relax and have a good time."

"This isn't a pleasure trip."

"Pretend."

"I'll *pretend* you didn't say that," Elizabeth lightly warned, then scooted out the passenger side of the car. She waved on her way to the front porch, past ever-blooming rose bushes.

Stepping into the living room, she looked beyond the dining-room doorway and saw her son sitting at the kitchen table. He glanced over at her before turning his attention back to the bowl in front of him.

Covering up a twinge of disappointment, she put on a bright smile as she headed toward him. "Hi, Brodie."

He muttered a response without lifting his gaze from his enormous serving of corn flakes.

"About last night," she began, realizing that she had to smooth things over between them before she left.

His hand tightened around the spoon. "I don't want to talk about it."

"Maybe not, but—"

"Grandma already told me nothing happened. So, did he."

"Max?"

After a moment's hesitation, Brodie answered, "Yeah. So there's nothing to talk about. Okay?" The awkward embarrassment written on her son's face stopped her from pursuing the issue further. "What are you doing home, anyway? Are you still tired?"

She detected a change of tone in his voice. "No. I'm not sick, either," she reassured him, then launched into a quick explanation. "Hey, I've got some great news! We've found a new water pump in Chicago. I'm flying up there this afternoon, but I won't be back until Monday night. So, you help your grandma with things around here while I'm gone, okay?"

"How come you're going for the whole weekend?"

Elizabeth felt her own awkward embarrassment come over her. After convincing her son that nothing had happened with Max, she was about to tell him that she was taking off with the same man for two whole nights.

"The only way to get that pump in time to do any good is to pick it up myself and fly it down here. The fastest way to do that is in Max Wilder's plane. He offered me a lift. Actually, it was Max who located the pump."

"Then let Wildman get the pump himself." Brodie shoved his chair back and headed for the back door.

CHAPTER 7

"HOLD IT RIGHT THERE, young man." Elizabeth dropped her purse on the table, prepared to go after her son if he didn't stop. He pulled up at the sound of her voice but didn't turn around. "What's wrong, Brodie?"

"Nothing." He shifted from one foot to the other. "I don't feel like talking right now. Can I go? There aren't any chores I have to do."

She mentally reached down into her much-depleted reserves of patience. His attitude was not a part of the son she knew. She crossed the kitchen and planted herself in front of him.

"What's gotten into you?" she asked but was met with little more than a shrug. "Mr. *Wilder* came back to Alton to help the flood victims, not to single-handedly save our old boarding house. I need his plane to bring back this water pump, but I don't expect him to buy it for us. Neither does Grandma. If I didn't go on this flight, however, she said she was going to."

"Grandma? But she's scared of flying."

"You know that and I know that. But she was bound and determined to pack her bags if I didn't agree to make the trip."

"That's all it is, then? Just a trip to get a water pump?"

"Yes." Elizabeth gently grasped his upper arms. "Give me a little credit, Brodie. I haven't seen Max in years. He's practically a stranger to me."

"He *was* your old boyfriend."

"Ancient history." *I hope.* "Max and I are nothing more than friends now. Got it?"

Though he nodded reluctantly, he didn't look convinced. "You wouldn't have to go to Chicago if those ladies could go to some other shelter."

"They can't, son." Elizabeth shook her head slowly. "Besides, that old boarding house has been in this family for generations. I've got to do everything I can to save it. And I need you to help me out here, Brodie. Your grandma already has enough on her mind, with the shelter and you two kids. She won't show it, but I know she's worried about my plane trip. I want you to be strong for her and Annie. Can I count on you?"

"Yeah, I guess so," he drawled. His lopsided grin gave her a glimmer of the sweet-faced little boy who had always melted her heart.

~

WHEN MAX ARRIVED to pick up Liza Jane, he was more than anxious to get started on their trip. In the two hours he'd given her, he finished some last-minute business, stopped by the boarding house to check on the ailing pump and made a couple phone calls. Even though Bernice appreciated his efforts to take Elizabeth out of town for a few days, she had given him a stern warning about taking good care of her daughter-in-law.

He fully intended to.

Smiling to himself, Max got out and walked around the front of the truck just as Liza Jane came down the front-porch steps with a small suitcase in her left hand, a light jacket and her purse in the other. She had changed out of her jeans and denim shirt, which would have been better suited for riding in his cargo plane. The gray slacks and soft pink print blouse belonged to the Elizabeth he didn't know.

"Ready?" he asked.

"Not really. I can't believe I let you talk me into this trip on such short notice. I'm not a spontaneous person."

"You used to be." Reaching for her suitcase, he ran his gaze down the length of her. Damned if she didn't set his blood churning in her fancy clothes. He looked back up to find her watching him. The wary expression in her eyes conveyed a cool warning. She knew him too well. He couldn't say the same about her. Not anymore. He tossed her bag in the truck bed, saying over his shoulder, "I don't remember the last time I bothered to clean the seats in my plane. So you better not whine if you get grease on those pants."

"I don't whine."

The memory of her at his bathroom door challenged him to make a remark, but he held his tongue. She was skittish enough about flying off with him for the weekend without being reminded of that hot little incident in the hallway. If he didn't keep his mouth shut, he would never get her out of the driveway, let alone onto the plane.

He opened the passenger door for her and helped her up into the cab. Not until she rolled down the window and waved toward the house did he notice her son standing behind the screen door. Brodie responded with a minimal raise of his hand, but no smile. Max wondered if the boy was still hot under the collar about last night or if things had been settled between him and his mom. When Max slid in behind the wheel, he noticed her enthusiastic expression falter for a flicker of a second.

"Is everything okay?" he asked.

Her eyebrows lifted with renewed optimism. "Yes, of course."

"You never did have a good poker face."

She gave him a sideways glance without meeting his gaze. "So, sue me."

He shifted the gears into reverse with a subdued chuckle, content to see the quick comeback of the old Liza Jane. In a strange way, he liked sparring with her. He was tempted to egg her on but thought better of it. They had a long weekend ahead and he didn't want her pulling back into her "Elizabeth" shell every time she caught herself being Liza Jane again. What he needed to do was let her slip back into those old, comfortable ways little by little, without tipping her off to how much he was enjoying himself—and enjoying her.

As for Brodie, Max wasn't surprised the kid was still angry. If roles were reversed, he'd feel the same. "Your son didn't seem very happy. Is he mad at you for going to Chicago with me?"

"No, not at all." His deliberate glance of disbelief made her shift nervously in her seat. "Well, not anymore. Concerned, maybe. About you... and me. I have a hunch it could have a little bit to do with John, too."

Max felt a twinge of jealousy over the mention of Johnny, but he managed to stuff it away, determined not to let it interfere with his weekend with Liza Jane.

When she explained about the whole family's fear of flying, he started worrying about her own feelings, her own memories of the horrible air disaster that had killed her husband. For a second, a picture of his best friend flashed in his mind. Max mentally shook off the image of a grinning teenager sitting on the fender of an old farm truck, a beer raised to the sky, singing like Billy Joel, "Only the good die young."

Max's knuckles tightened around the steering wheel. He hated thinking about Johnny being gone, never mind how he died. Max allowed himself a quick sideways look at Liza Jane. Now here he was taking her up in his big old Beech-17, the furthest thing from a commercial jet short of borrowing the *Spirit of Saint Louis* from the Smithsonian.

"I think now's as good a time as any to warn you that my plane doesn't sport all that insulation, all the frills of one of those passenger jobs. It's noisy and cold at higher altitude. But I've been over every inch of her, inside and out. She's been inspected by the best. I take real good care of her, so there's nothing for you to worry about."

"When I mentioned my family's fear, I never said I was worried, did I?"

"No, but—"

"Do I *look* worried?"

He glanced over at her, sitting on her side of the cab seat, her posture a little too stiff even for Elizabeth. "Yep."

"Well, I'm not."

"If you say so."

"I do."

~

DURING THE FIRST SEVERAL MINUTES in the air, Elizabeth gripped the seat cushion beneath her, her fear of flying barely under control. Unwilling to let Max see the tension in her face, she turned her head toward the window, pretending she was fascinated with the view. All she saw was murky brown water, covering endless miles of what had once been small towns and farms. She was stunned. The aerial view encompassed the massive flood that could not be captured by television screens and newspaper photos.

The flood in 1993 had nearly taken the historic boarding house, as Bernice was fond of saying, but the citizens of Alton managed the pumps and filled sandbags to hold back the Mississippi until it crested that first Sunday in August. Would this be the year that they lost the old building?

The pump should hold until Monday, she told herself—if only the rain lets up. But the weatherman held out little hope for such a miracle. From the look of the clouds up ahead, rain was already belting down in central Illinois. Max had been right about trying to beat the storm instead of flying to Chicago on Monday.

She swallowed hard, pushing back the thought of losing her battle with the river as the plane shuddered. She swallowed again and glanced nervously at Max, dislodging the enormous headphones on her ears as she did so. She pushed them back into place.

Despite the convenience of the electronic communication system that linked them, he raised his voice over the engine noise to speak into the tiny microphone positioned in front of his mouth.

"Turbulence," he explained without a hint of concern.

Even though he'd given her fair warning, Elizabeth wasn't prepared for the stark reality of the sparse accommodations. There were only two small seats—for the pilot and a single passenger—inside the cavernous cargo plane. Even though they sat a few feet apart, the droning roar inside the metal shell made conversation impossible without the headphones and mics. To make matters worse, they were headed into a wall of dark clouds.

"Are we flying through *that?*"

He nodded, looking a little too self-assured even for "Wildman" Wilder. She suspected it was all an act for her sake.

Her headphones shifted again. She fixed them nervously, trying to hold down the queasy feeling that crept up her throat. Within moments, they found themselves surrounded by flashes of lightning, buffeted by winds. When the plane went through a particularly bad bit of turbulence, she reached out to grab hold of something, anything, to brace herself.

Everything was metal. She pulled her hand back. They were a flying lightning rod!

Another wave of nausea rolled upward with the dip and tilt of the plane.

"Where's the restroom?" she yelled over the noise. A boom of thunder drowned out his response. "What?"

"No bathroom on board."

"What?"

"I said—"

"I heard you!" She glanced around the floor at her feet, then twisted in her seat to look behind her. The headphones fell off. Another series of bumps jolted her, but the seat belt kept her from being tossed onto the floor. If she didn't find an airsick bag, nothing was going to keep her from humiliating herself in front of him.

She fumbled with the antiquated buckle. If she had to lose her lunch, she would at least throw up somewhere in the back of the plane.

Over the drone of engines and thunder, she heard him holler, "Where are you going?"

She didn't answer, clapping her hand over her mouth as she dashed out of her seat.

∾

"Are you sure you're alright?" Max asked for at least the tenth time during the rest of the flight and after the uneventful landing at a municipal airport outside Chicago.

"I'll be good as new now that we're on solid ground." As she walked across the tarmac with him, she welcomed the gentle support of his arm around her waist, despite the achingly familiar effect it had on her from stirred memories of the past. Even though she could probably walk well enough on her own, it felt good to lean on someone else for a little while.

But only for a little while, she reminded herself, paying a small token of attention to the voice inside that warned against displaying this or any other sort of weakness to Max Wilder. She couldn't let go of a need to prove she was perfectly capable of taking care of herself. Sure, she was the one who had looked him up when she needed his help to fix the pump. And, yes, she was glad that he had tracked down a replacement. Of course she appreciated his offer to fly her here to buy it. But she didn't like how easily she let him take over. Like right now.

Elizabeth felt the warmth of his arm clasping her waist—supporting her, protecting her. Possessing her. When this unnerving thought struck her, she withdrew her arm from around him, saying quietly, "I really don't need any more help."

Approaching the curb in front of the small terminal building, Max smiled. "Good, he's here."

"Who?"

He gestured with a swoop of his hand toward a man in a black suit standing beside a long, sleek black Mercedes limousine. "Our chauffeur."

Elizabeth stood speechless as Max spoke with the driver, who then stepped to the rear passenger door and swung it open. "If you'll please leave your luggage on the curb, ma'am, I'll be happy to place it in the trunk. You too, sir."

She slowly turned to Max, eyeing him suspiciously. "What's going on?"

"Oh... nothing," he drawled as a corner of his mouth tilted into a lazy smile.

She hooked her thumb toward the car. "This luxury limo is *nothing*? I know I'm going to regret asking, but what's this all about?"

His cocky grin melted into a serious expression. "It's about making the most of two short days away from that godforsaken flood." He held up his hand, halting any argument from her. "Now don't go getting defensive about me spending a few dollars on you."

"But you really didn't need to spend—"

"Never mind what I'm spending. It's only money, Liza Jane. I have more than I need. Let me do this for you."

Thoughts of hailing a cab darted through her brain until she dismissed the idea as being too reactionary. After all, it was just a limousine, for heaven's sake. Not a red-carpet ride into sin and debauchery. She was simply overreacting to warning bells that went off every time he was around.

Max didn't miss the subtle change in her as they stood side by side. He also noticed the way she managed to put a few extra inches between them. Her wall was back up again.

Goodbye for now, Liza Jane.

Ending the long, silent standoff, she sighed heavily in defeat and headed toward the open passenger door.

Max had wanted her to enjoy the luxury of a chauffeur-driven limousine for their ride into the city, where life went on as if no one knew about a mammoth flood taking place in their backyard. He'd wanted her eyes to pop when the limo pulled up in front of the classy hotel. He'd wanted her jaw to drop as she entered the luxurious two-bedroom suite.

When they finally stood alone in the suite, his hand swept wide to encompass the richly decorated sitting room. "What do you think?"

"It's... nice. Very nice." She glanced around, then turned and faced him, clearly uncomfortable. "*Too* nice... for me, anyway. But I'm sure it must grow on you after a while. It's funny, but after seeing you back in Alton, I just assumed from the way you dressed... that is, you seem so normal."

"The money hasn't changed me."

"I didn't think it had. Until now."

"This isn't how I live, Liza Ja—Elizabeth." His stumbling effort to correct himself brought a small smile from her that quickly faded.

She walked to the sofa, but remained standing, silently taking it all in. She looked pale and fragile as she crossed her arms under her small breasts. Her gaze dropped to the glass-topped coffee table and the floral centerpiece of fresh red roses and white daisies. He watched her reach down for the little white envelope stuck into the arrangement. Max came up beside her while she read the message.

He had the strongest urge to take the card from her and say what was in his heart rather than the "Love, Max" that had been jotted down by a florist. Damned if he could come up with the right things to say, no matter how many times he went over them in his head. For now, he hoped the flowers would convey his feelings. That he cared for her. That he wanted to give her something beautiful. That this was only the beginning of all the things he wanted to give to her.

"Thank you." Her voice was barely above a whisper. "But I wish you hadn't gone to all this trouble. The limo, this suite, and now these flowers..."

"Just pretend you're Cinderella for the weekend."

"And what are you? My fairy godmother?"

"Hardly." He laughed. "I think I'll stick to playing the knight in shining armor."

"I appreciate your efforts, Max, but I'm not cut out to be a pampered princess."

"Don't sell yourself short," he gently scolded, then took her hand and led her toward a doorway. "Before you get on your high horse and head out looking for a budget motel, I want you to see something."

As he stepped into one of the bedrooms, she held back and pulled her hand free. He looked over his shoulder and saw wariness in her green eyes.

Without a hint of anger or accusation, she simply stated, "I can see right through all of this, Max. You planned every last detail so that we'd spend the rest of the weekend in bed together."

He cocked his head. "Seems you already got your mind made up. No sense in ruining your picture of me with a bit of truth now, is there?"

"Quit trying to bluff me, Max. I know what you're up to."

"Believe it or not, kid, you haven't got a clue." He went to the closet, opened the door and yanked some clothes off their hangers. After tossing four evening gowns across the king-size bed, he pointed at them.

"These are the *only* things I bought that are going to end up on this bed. I might be filthy rich Liza Jane, but I've never used my money to buy a woman. And I'm not about to start now. This weekend is not about sex. All I wanted to do was take you away from that damn flood for a few days."

"That's all?"

CHAPTER 8

"*D*ON'T LOOK SO STUNNED." Max couldn't blame her for being suspicious of his motives. But, dammit, he meant every word. He wanted to wine and dine her like she deserved. "Just do me a favor and pick out a dress."

He watched her hold up a shimmering, metallic-blue mini-dress—the tiniest of the four.

"This will never fit." She shook her head, then gazed at the remaining gowns. "I don't think any of them will fit. How did you ever...?"

"A few phone calls and a concierge who went above and beyond the call of duty."

He picked up a silver, sequined number with a long slit up one side. His imagination ran wild, picturing a sultry image of Liza Jane and a stimulating glimpse of her slender legs. He ignored the rush of desire, but his voice didn't sound as steady as he would have liked. "And yes, these should fit. Mrs. Mac gave me your sizes—all of them. There are shoes to match each one of the dresses."

"I don't know what Bernice was thinking." Elizabeth shook her head. "These things are tiny."

"So are you."

"Not like this." She held the dress up against her body. "I could never squeeze into it."

"I say you're wrong." Admiring the view, he silently admitted the dress would certainly fit her like a second skin, but that's how it was designed.

"Wrong? About the dress size? Are you kidding?"

"Not at all. I'm even willing to bet that every one of these will fit you like a glove."

Elizabeth studied his deliciously dark eyes, which held a hint of challenge. He looked a bit too smug for his own good. "What are the stakes?"

"If these don't fit, I'll leave you alone for the entire weekend. You can stop worrying that I'm going to coax you into bed. I'll give you my room key and you won't see me until Monday morning."

"This whole suite? All to myself?"

He nodded.

"Without you?"

Again, he nodded, but this time with an expression of rejection etched across his forehead. She expected as much from him. It was her own sense of disappointment that disturbed her. Unwilling to admit that a weekend of solitude would be anything less than appealing, she stated, "I could just as easily enjoy myself at a moderately priced hotel using my own credit card."

"With room service? And this view? I don't think so."

He had her there. The luxurious suite was something out of a fairy tale. Somewhere in the far reaches of her brain, she felt a long-forgotten part of herself coming back to life, the part of her that grabbed hold of the moment and ran with it. For a split second, she felt the giddy exhilaration of accepting a dare, of taking a challenge. Just as quickly, she clamped down on such nonsense. Max was playing a game with her. He was too confident to make a bet with her that he couldn't win. He was simply waiting for her to take the bait.

"And if these things fit me... what do *you* get out of it?"

One corner of his mouth tilted up. "You."

His blunt declaration hung in the air between them for an eternity. His audacity amused her, much to her own surprise. It also did a lot of other things to her that she had no business thinking about. Keeping a close check on her feelings around Max was a full-time job. Trying hard to contain her smile of amusement, Elizabeth slowly shook her head and dropped the blue dress on top of the others.

"Those stakes are too high for me. I'm out."

As she turned toward the door, his hand lightly touched her shoulder.

"Wait, Liza Jane." The husky whisper raked across the fragile surface of her emotions. She looked down at his fingertips. A mere touch, but, oh what it did to every muscle, every nerve ending. She didn't dare move, unable to trust her precarious balancing act between the past and present, between what once was and what was never meant to be again.

"Don't ask me for what I can't give, Max. I won't do it. I promised—" She cut off the rest of the sentence, damning herself for allowing such a slip of the tongue. No one could know. Least of all Max.

Elizabeth almost made it to the bedroom door before his words stopped her in mid-step.

"No sex."

She pivoted. "Say that again?"

"This weekend isn't about sex."

"Then what is it about?" She glanced around the suite, at the exquisite designer dresses lying on the bed. "Do you lavish every woman with this kind of attention, then pat her on the head and send her back home at the end of the weekend?"

He chuckled. "You're the only one."

"And I'm supposed to be grateful?"

"A little."

She studied him with a level gaze. What was he up to? "If sex isn't your motive behind this plush suite and these fancy clothes, then what is?"

As he walked over to her, the playful smile on his face faded, replaced by an expression so intense, so serious her heart began to pound. No more games, she realized. No more jokes and innuendos. She couldn't decide whether to turn tail and run, or to stay and be swept away again.

He stopped in front of her, yet he didn't touch her, didn't reach out for her. She silently thanked him for that, certain she would have let the last of her resolve drop away if she'd felt the slightest contact with him.

She slowly lifted her face to look up into his dark blue eyes. His heated gaze penetrated her cool facade, flowing past every barrier like lava melting everything in its path. Hot desire pooled in the pit of her belly.

"I want you, Elizabeth."

Here it comes, she thought, damning the weakness in her knees and the weakness in her heart.

"I want you," he repeated, "but not this way. I want to start over. I want to take you out on the town. I want to see you relax and have a good time. No pressure. No expectations at the end of the evening. Let's pretend we never met before tonight. And when we come back to the suite, I'll kiss you good-night at your door—if you'll let me—and I'll walk down the hall to my own room. Tomorrow we'll go to a movie, a museum or whatever you pick. In the evening, we'll do up the town again—same song, second verse. What do you say?"

She took a moment to find her voice. "I must be crazy to let you talk me into this."

His lips slowly lifted in a grin of triumph. "Be ready by seven?"

"Only if the dresses fit," she reminded him, nodding toward the bed. He didn't take his eyes off her, confidence radiating from him like a heat wave.

"See you at seven."

Before she could utter another word, he stepped around her and headed down the hall to the second bedroom without a backward glance.

~

MAX STOOD IN FRONT of the bathroom mirror, fumbling with the black bow tie for the hundredth time. He could take apart an engine with the dexterity of a surgeon, but tonight he couldn't seem to make his fingers do anything right. He checked his watch. Five minutes to seven.

"Get a move on, Wilder," he muttered, trying one more time to get the tie straight. Finally succeeding, he glared at his reflection in the black tuxedo and shook his head in disbelief. At least he looked a hell of a lot more at ease in the penguin suit than he felt. Hopefully, Liza Jane would be so dazzled by his appearance that she wouldn't notice he was as nervous as a high school kid on prom night. Back in those days, however, he never experienced this jittery anticipation before a date with Liza Jane. If anything, he had looked forward to the end of their evening with eager hormones. Tonight would be different, though.

Max was out to win her heart. He wanted to know what love could really be like with Liza Jane. He was banking everything on this night, this weekend. For years, he had dreamed of a second chance, but had long ago given up believing it would ever happen. Now it was here, staring him right in the face.

"Who am I kidding?" He stared at his reflection. Wanting to

make a good impression, he looked more like a Thanksgiving turkey on a silver platter. Liza Jane would take one look at him and laugh herself silly. Mentally dismissing the image of total humiliation, he swiped his hand across the light switch on his way out of the room.

By the time he knocked on her door, he had convinced himself that the evening might possibly turn out to be a disaster. But every thought, every concern flew out of his head as the door slowly opened, revealing the breathtaking picture of a slinky, sophisticated lady in shimmering silver. Her casual upsweep of dark blond hair left delicate wisps around a face that belonged on the cover of a high-class fashion magazine. Thick, dark lashes and sultry shadow around her eyes deepened the exotic green color until his blood ran hot and his temperature skyrocketed. Gone was the teenage Liza Jane. Gone was the straitlaced Elizabeth.

"Well, say something," she pleaded with a lilt of nervous laughter.

His eyes raked over her with unabashed appreciation.

"Wow."

She chuckled, self-consciously skimming her hand across her flat stomach. "It looks like you won the bet."

"Disappointed?"

Her dark, moist lips moved tantalizingly into a slight smile before she whispered, "No."

He was certain she had no idea that her body language was driving him crazy. Her innocence added to the allure. If only he could close the bedroom door behind him and take her in his arms. If only he could show her how much he wanted her at that very moment. It took every ounce of strength to keep from reaching out to her. Instead, he stepped back and gestured down the hallway toward the door of the suite.

"Shall we go, Cinderella?"

As she walked past him, she eyed him suspiciously, despite the glint of amusement in her eyes. "What do you have planned?"

"It's a surprise." Following her, he admired the gentle sway of her slender hips. "Besides, half the fun is in the anticipation."

She glanced back over her shoulder and caught him gazing at her backside. "And just exactly what are you anticipating, Max?"

"Nothing," he said, playing dumb. "Nothing at all."

~

FROM THE MOMENT HE ESCORTED LIZA JANE through the lobby of the hotel to the waiting limousine at the curb, their evening on the town took on a magic all its own. Max had meticulously planned every detail, being sure to take her to the best restaurant with the most spectacular view of the city. Afterward, they stopped at a fancy nightclub, where she turned every head in the crowd. Over the course of the evening, he watched her apprehension slowly dissolve as the Cinderella fantasy pushed aside her real-life worries. The stroke of midnight would come soon enough—on Monday morning. Until then, he would do everything in his power to make her radiantly happy.

Returning to the penthouse at three in the morning, Max stood close to Liza Jane at the open doorway of her bedroom. He gazed down into her upturned face, fighting his desire to make love to her.

"Thank you, Max." A soft rasp in her tired voice made him think of waking up next to her in the morning, of kissing her and making her moan. "It was all so wonderful."

"Yeah... wonderful," he repeated in a daze, his mind filled with intimate thoughts of this beautiful woman lying beneath him. "I hate for it to end."

He lowered his mouth to hers. She tilted her head, allowing him to give her a soft, gentle kiss. When her subtle perfume filled his senses, Max slipped his arms around her waist and rested his hands on her bottom.

"It doesn't need to end yet," he murmured, then brushed his lips against hers and found them stiff and unresponsive. Realizing his mistake, he silently cursed a blue streak for his behavior. "I'm sorry. I didn't mean—"

She moved out of the circle of his embrace, a weak smile faltering as she shook her head. "No, it was my fault. I misled you to think—"

"Cut it out, Liza Jane. You didn't do anything wrong, dammit. It was me, okay? I promised you this weekend wasn't about sex and I meant it."

He could see the distrust in her eyes. The progress he had made with her during the evening had vanished, destroyed by his one wrong move. Letting out a long sigh of self-loathing, he reached up and rubbed the back of his neck as he shook his head in disgust. With his other hand, he withdrew the room key-card from his pocket and handed it to her.

"Bet's off. I'll grab my bag and check into another room."

"Don't leave." Her frown deepened. "Not on account of me. It was a... misunderstanding. Besides, it's three in the morning. You won't be able to get a room at this hour."

"I'm sure I can find somebody at the front desk to help me. If not—" he shrugged somewhat dramatically "—I'll take a walk."

"You'll do no such thing!"

"The fresh air will do me good."

"You could get mugged."

"Are you worried?"

"Yes... No." She squared her shoulders and tilted her chin to look up at him. "Okay, so I'd be a little worried—"

"Aha! You *do* care about me."

She held up her hand. "You didn't let me finish. I would be worried about finding another pilot to fly the water pump back to Alton."

Her admission brought a small smile to his lips.

"Go to your room, Max."

"Are you sure?"

"Don't worry about your carnal impulses—I'll lock my door and prop a chair under the doorknob."

He grinned at the sarcastic quip, reminiscent of the old days. "Good night, Liza Jane."

"Night, Max," she said, stepping into her room and flipping a wall switch to the right of the door. A soft glow of lamplight illuminated the peach walls behind her. "Sleep well."

"Not a chance."

As the door shut, he heard her soft chuckle, then silence. He waited. Finally, Max tapped on the door.

"Yes?"

"The lock."

"Oh... yes, of course." The distinctive dick echoed in the quiet hallway.

Max grinned. "Thank you," he said through the closed door.

"You're welcome."

Silence fell once again. Max knew she was standing on the other side, waiting. He lifted his hand to knock, then stopped, touching the center of the door with his fingertips.

Elizabeth held her breath, wishing she could drag herself away from the locked door, yet unable to make her legs move. She listened for footsteps. Even though the carpet would muffle the sound, she was certain he hadn't left.

She felt his presence in every fiber of her being. She had experienced the very same sensation earlier in the evening. Whenever he left her side for a moment, she sensed his return before she turned to see him. Something like a ripple of electricity had passed through her. The feeling was thrilling, yet eerie at the same time. She felt it now. The air practically vibrated with an inaudible hum that penetrated her body.

What are you doing to me, Max? Why didn't I take your key? Why didn't I let you leave when I had the chance?

She tightened both hands at her sides, curling her fingers into clenched fists, battling her temptation to open the door. She couldn't break her promise to herself. She would not go back to Max. Physical desire be damned. She wasn't a kid anymore.

She shut her eyes and concentrated on pushing him from her mind, as if sheer mental will could force him to walk away.

The ring of her bedside phone startled her.

Aware of the early hour, Elizabeth immediately thought of her family in flood-ravaged Alton. Suppressing a wave of panic, she dashed across the room and picked up the receiver.

"Mom?" Her son's voice was calm yet laced with tension.

"Brodie, what's wrong?"

"I've been calling you nearly every hour. Didn't you get my messages?"

Elizabeth felt a wave of guilt as she glanced down at the blinking light on her phone. "No, I was out."

"Until three o'clock?" he asked incredulously.

"Yes, son." Elizabeth sensed the directions of his thoughts, running rampant with the wrong ideas about her evening with Max. "What's this all about?"

"The pump went out about eight last night."

She gripped the receiver. "How bad is it?"

"The basement's filling up fast. All the women are packing up their stuff, to get ready to leave. But they don't have any place to go."

"Let me talk to your grandmother."

"She's at the boarding house. I offered to help, but she didn't want Annie to wake up and find the house empty. Might freak her out."

"I'm glad you're there to take care of your sister."

He muttered something incomprehensible, dismissing her praise. "How soon can you get back?"

Elizabeth hesitated. She could not do any more than Bernice was already doing. Still, her conscience would never give her a moment's peace if she stayed in Chicago for the rest of the weekend. If she hopped the next plane for Saint Louis, Max could pick up the pump on Monday and fly it home. They would still need it for cleanup efforts after the floodwater receded.

"Mom? Are you still there?"

"Yes, honey, I'm still here." She glanced toward the bedroom door, then turned her attention back to the phone. "Let Grandma know you reached me and tell her I'm on my way."

"When do you think you'll get here?"

"I won't know until I call the airlines."

As soon as she hung up, there was a light knock, followed by the concerned voice of Max. "Elizabeth? I heard the phone ring. Is everything okay?"

She unlocked the door and opened it. His tie hung loose around the open collar of his tuxedo shirt, which was unbuttoned halfway down his chest. From the disheveled look of him, he must have started undressing on his way to his room.

"Brodie called. The pump gave out last night. Bernice is evacuating the women and children. I told him I'd fly home today."

"What's the point? By the time you get there, everybody will already be at the Red Cross shelter."

"No, Bernice wouldn't do that." Her terse answer surprised him. "That is, she... well, it's not exactly that easy to explain."

"I'm all ears." He stepped into her room.

Elizabeth backed away, then turned and walked to the bank of windows overlooking the city. The open drapes allowed the city lights to filter in through sheer white curtains. She parted them and gazed at taxis and delivery trucks crisscrossing the streets below.

"Funny how something that started out with such good intentions could turn into such a big secret." She pivoted to look at him across the room. She rubbed her palms together nervously.

His dark eyebrows drew together as he watched her intently. "Are you mixed up in something illegal?"

"No, not at all," she quickly explained. "I suppose I can trust you...."

"At this stage, you're going to have to."

CHAPTER 9

*E*LIZABETH PRESSED HER FINGERTIPS to her temple in an effort to make herself think straight. "This isn't going very well at all."

"Then spit it out," Max said.

"The McKenzie boarding house is actually a women's shelter for victims of domestic violence."

"Well, I'll be damned. Bernice finally got to do it."

"Do it? You mean the shelter?"

"Yeah. I remember Johnny telling me that his mom wanted to open a home for women like her who didn't have anywhere to go."

"You knew about her abusive husband?"

He nodded solemnly. Johnny's old man lived in Saint Louis. I drove down with Johnny to visit him a couple times, before his old man died of cancer in our senior year. Too much booze. He was an okay guy until he drank."

"I don't think Bernice ever stopped loving him, even after she found the courage to leave him."

"Wouldn't he be surprised if he knew his family's historic

boarding house was a women's shelter? Those ladies and their kids are really in hiding?"

"Yes. They came from areas in and around Saint Louis. We are far enough from their neighborhoods to offer some degree of protection. For their own safety, we don't identify the McKenzie house as a shelter."

Comprehension dawned on him as he nodded in agreement. "I suppose if word got around, it might be risky. But for now, couldn't they go to a local flood-relief shelter without worrying about an abusive husband or boyfriend tracking them down?"

Elizabeth shook her head. "Haven't you seen the news media swarming into Alton to cover the floods? They look everywhere to interview flood victims. The TV news could air a clip with one of our women. Even if they are only in the background, a husband or boyfriend could see it. Or they could be told about it."

"I understand your concern."

"So you can see that I must go home to find the women temporary housing until the boardinghouse is available again."

He rubbed his neck. "No, what I see is that you're not giving Bernice enough credit to come up with her own solution to the problem."

"That's not true, Max. I feel responsible."

"Why? You are not the one who brought on these floods. You are not to blame for that pump dying. Why are you trying to save the world all by yourself, Liza Jane?"

"I'm not. I'm only trying to help a handful of people." Avoiding his piercing gaze, she glanced around the spacious bedroom.

"But you don't have to do it alone," he said in a strained tone. "Bernice has been a tough-minded, independent lady a lot longer than you've been on this earth. Maybe she doesn't need you to come to her rescue. Did you ever think of that?"

Elizabeth sighed heavily, realizing it was useless to argue with Max. He wanted her to stay. Nothing she could say would convince him that she needed to be at home in Alton. She needed to be with her family. Not just Annie, Brodie and Bernice, but with her new extended family—people she cared about at the shelter.

"I never should have come with you this weekend," she said quietly. "Brodie was right."

"About what?" Suspicion shadowed Max's face.

"Brodie wanted me to stay home and let you pick up the new pump alone. I'm inclined to think he was right, after all. This was a mistake. How could I have flown off on the spur of the moment and abandoned everybody in the middle of this disaster?"

Max crossed the room and took her by the shoulders. "Are you telling me that Brodie tried to stop you from taking this trip?"

"Yes, but—"

"But nothing. He's got you jumping on the first plane out of here."

"Are you saying that he's lied about the basement flooding?"

"No." He loosened his grasp and let his hands slide down her slender arms. "Exaggerated a little."

"Not Brodie. You don't know him. He's not like that." Her jaw tightened.

Max was pushing her and he knew it. But he had to make her see that her son could still be angry enough to pull this kind of stunt, especially if it meant dragging her back from Chicago. And away from him.

"Call Bernice. Ask her if it's as bad as Brodie says."

"No." Elizabeth withdrew from Max, folding her arms in front of her. "I trust my son and I don't need Bernice to prove he is not making all of this up."

"Fine," he answered reluctantly, with a shrug. "But you could call to ask if she's located a place for the women and children. That wouldn't be questioning your son's integrity, would it?"

"No." He sensed her resistance might be slipping, but only slightly.

He went over to the telephone on her bedside table, picked up the receiver and held it out to her. She didn't move. Instead, she stood at the window, her shimmery silver dress silhouetted against the city lights. He stared at the phone in his hand. "I think you're relieved to have an excuse to run back home."

The full brunt of his remark stunned Elizabeth. In silence, she slowly turned around and pinned him with a cold stare. "Let me get this straight... I'm supposed to be relieved that their misery is bailing me out of a weekend with you?"

"Not when you put it that way."

"Is there another way?"

Max hung up the receiver, then shoved his hands in his pockets. "I'm too damn tired to fight over a phone call. If the situation is as bad as Brodie says, don't you think Mrs. Mac would have left a message for you?"

She gave a curt nod at the blinking light on the telephone. "Maybe she did. Maybe Brodie wasn't the only one trying to reach me all night long."

"Care to find out?"

Without another word, Elizabeth went to the bedside table, sat down on the edge of the bed and retrieved all the electronic messages.

"Nothing from Bernice?" Max asked as she hung up, his tone a little too self-righteous.

Her head jerked up. "That doesn't mean there isn't a real emergency."

"Maybe..." He stepped closer. She craned her neck to look up at him. "Then again, maybe not."

Elizabeth grew uncomfortable with his imposing height towering over her. If she stood up now, she would be right where he wanted her—within easy reach. It would take so little to convince her to stay with him for the rest of the weekend. She was already treading on thin ice.

And the thought of giving in to him scared the hell out of her.

Was she looking for an excuse to run? Was she relieved to have an emergency to call her home? The questions in her own mind disturbed her more than the accusations coming from Max.

Her gaze drifted to the bedside table. One phone call. That's all she needed to prove to herself as well as Max that she wasn't running from him.

As she reached for the receiver, she paused. "If Bernice tells me she's evacuating the shelter, nothing is going to stop me from going home."

"Understood."

Elizabeth punched in the familiar number of the McKenzie boarding house.

"The line's busy." With a frustrated sigh, she hung up. "Maybe she's trying to reach me."

"So we'll wait."

She checked her watch. "Five minutes."

He sat down next to her on the edge of the bed. She resisted the urge to shy away from him, to put some distance between them. Restless, she glanced at her watch again, then at the sleek dress barely covering her thighs.

With a discreet movement of her hand, she tugged at the hem.

Max spoke in a calmer voice. "Why don't you change clothes? I'll listen for the phone so you can get ready to leave."

"You don't mind?"

"Sitting by the phone, no. Your leaving, yes." He leaned forward, resting his forearms on his knees. The white French cuffs set off the deep tan of his hands as he intertwined his long fingers. Unwelcome memories rushed through her mind—memories of his touch, memories of her heated response. A swirl of warmth spiraled into her belly as she recalled their passionate lovemaking of long ago.

Stop this! Despite the silent reprimand, a physical ache remained in the wake of the powerful image. Closing her eyes, she reached up and lightly pinched the bridge of her nose, trying to shut out the past.

"Headache?" Max asked, drawing her out of her disturbing thoughts.

"Sort of." The little white lie was better than confessing her thoughts about the one thing she did not want to happen between them.

His left hand slid across her bare back and gently cupped her shoulder. His thumb lightly rested on the back of her neck. She didn't want to like it as much as she did.

"I kept you out too late." His thumb began to move slowly back and forth in a lulling caress. She attempted to smile, but yawned sleepily instead.

"I—I haven't stayed up all night since Annie was a baby. She would snooze all day, then fuss until dawn. I was a sleep-deprived zombie for months."

"You really love being a mother."

"More than anything in the world." Her eyes grew moist with unexpected emotion, no doubt a result of her exhaustion. "It's an incredible feeling to simply have this love that doesn't require anything from anybody. No strings attached. Nothing can destroy it. It's just there... in my heart."

"I envy you."

"Don't." She turned slightly and found his dark blue eyes riveted on her. "Just tell me that you're happy for me."

The words slipped out before she realized it. She dropped her gaze, quickly adding, "I don't know why I said that. I don't expect you to—"

The touch of his fingertip under her chin stopped her, tilting her head up.

"I *am* happy for you." Filled with quiet respect, his low voice seemed to resonate in the air between them, touching a chord deep within her. As a tear trickled down her cheek, she reached up to brush it away. Max caught her hand in his. She watched him open her fingers, then lower his head and press a kiss into her palm. The sensation of his breath on her skin sent a ripple of raw desire throughout her body.

She was so close to the edge, so dangerously close. Her mind spun with the dizziness of looking down from a mile-high precipice. Her heart rate quickened. She knew his next move as surely as she knew her own name. He would kiss her until all her good sense flew out the window, just like the unforgettable incident in his upstairs hallway.

"I... think it's been five minutes," she said weakly, dragging her hand from his grasp. The dark, smoldering look in his eyes held her gaze for a long moment, tempting her, drawing her closer. Barely able to find her voice, she could only whisper in a raspy breath, "What are you doing to me, Max?"

"It's not me." His gaze traveled from her forehead to her chin, lingering on her mouth before returning to her eyes. "It's us. You and me together. It's always been there."

His thumb on her neck continued its mesmerizing motion as Max moved closer. Elizabeth felt his other hand slip around her waist. Part of her wanted him to kiss her and hold her and make her feel alive again.

It's us. You and me together. It's always been there.

As he brushed his lips across hers, she drew back. His warm breath mingled with her own as she said softly, "I felt something for you once, Max. But please don't assume I've been holding on to those feelings all these years, especially while I was married to someone else."

"Not just someone else," he answered, his eyes filled with a sadness that tore through her. "My best friend... God, how I wish you knew how it felt to lay awake thinking of you with Johnny."

"Don't, Max. Don't bring it all up again. We've already said everything that needed to be said. I can't change the past." She paused, gazing intently into his pain-filled eyes. "And I realized a long time ago that I wouldn't have changed a thing. We were never meant to be together."

"No, I don't believe it." His hands tightened behind her neck and at her waist without posing a threat. "Maybe Johnny *was* the best thing that could've happened to you back then. But what about now, Liza Jane? Do you really think he would've wanted you to stop living? He's gone, but I'm here. Can't you give me—us —a second chance?"

"I wish I could," she answered, her voice barely audible.

"You *can* if you want to.... *Do* you?"

Elizabeth felt the gnawing hunger inside her, unable to deny the purely physical attraction she felt for Max. But what if that's all this was? "I just don't know."

"I'll accept that as a maybe, if you don't mind."

His hopeful half smile touched her in a way that was sweeter than words. She began to reach up, wanting to brush her fingertips across his cheek. But if she acted upon this one small temptation, she might not be able to stop herself from going further. Slowly she lowered her hand.

"I'm willing to wait as long as you need."

"Patience was never your strong suit."

His smile broadened. "I've learned that some things are worth waiting for."

In an effort to steer their conversation onto safer ground, Elizabeth gave a quick nod toward the nearby phone. "I'd better try Bernice again."

"Yeah. Right." Max dropped his hands to his sides and levered himself off the bed. Keeping his distance from Liza Jane was going to be the second hardest thing he had ever done. But not nearly as hard as those first few years living with the misery of losing her to Johnny.

He drew a deep breath and absently patted his chest for a pack of cigarettes that didn't exist. He shook his head at his lapse in memory, and his persistent desire for a smoke whenever he was around Liza Jane. She didn't make him want to pick up his old habit. It was how he felt around her, like a nervous tomcat on the prowl. He needed something to calm him down.

"The line's still busy," she said as she hung up. Max turned around and saw the worried expression on her face. "Do you suppose there's something wrong with the phone?"

"It's possible, especially if the flooded basement knocked out the power." Her deepening frown drew him back to her. He took her hands and brought her to her feet. "Why don't you get a few hours' sleep? Set your alarm for six. Call Bernice and tell her that you'll be taking the first flight to Saint Louis. I'll have room service deliver breakfast about six-thirty. What do you like? Eggs? Pancakes? Belgian waffles?"

"Toast and coffee."

"You'll need to have something solid to eat. You barely touched your swordfish last night."

"You're beginning to sound like Bernice."

He recalled the conversation between the two women in the kitchen of the boardinghouse. "And do you ever listen to her?"

Elizabeth opened her mouth to answer, but was interrupted by the ringing of the telephone. Max picked up the receiver and handed it to her.

"Hello...?" She glanced up at him, surprise in her green eyes. "Bernice! Where are you?... At home? Did Brodie give you my message?... Yes, I'm coming back right away. Max understands. He's staying until Monday to get the pump."

Max watched the exchange. Hearing only one side of the discussion put him at a disadvantage, but he was still able to figure out that Liza Jane was getting an argument from her mother-in-law. Her words suddenly became somewhat evasive, as if she was trying to avoid discussing him in his presence. Just what was it they were talking about, anyway?

Liza Jane looked up at him, though she spoke into the

receiver. "I can't speak for Max.... No, he's not here with me, Bernice. It's three-thirty, for heaven's sake. I'm sure he's sound asleep in his own room."

She lifted her eyebrows in a sheepish apology. Max felt a grin tug at the corner of his mouth as he slowly shook his head at her white lie. She shrugged impishly.

"Where are the women now?... *Our* house? All of them?... I suppose Annie and Brodie could give up their rooms and spend a few nights with friends... No, I don't mind at all. I will find a bigger place for everyone as soon as I get home... Yes, I *am* coming home. Leave Teresa and her kids in my room, and I'll share with you... No, you are not sleeping on the floor! Now, Bernice, this is ridiculous."

She gave Max a helpless look of frustration. He reached for the receiver, but she vigorously shook her head while batting his hand away.

"Yes, but—" Her words were cut off once more. "Bernice, listen to me. I'll be home before noon. I'm sure there's a better way to resolve this situation."

Max held up his index finger to get Elizabeth's attention, but she paid him no mind.

"I'll drive them to another shelter in the Saint Louis area," she told her mother-in-law. Max waggled two fingers in front of her eyes but she turned her head aside to avoid the distraction.

"No, I don't—"

He gently but firmly took the phone from her hand. "Bernice? This is Max."

After a brief moment of silence on the line, the woman bluntly replied, "Maxwell Wilder, you better talk some sense into that girl."

He grinned at Liza Jane, who looked about ready to murder him. "Yes, ma'am, I'm trying to do just that."

"She doesn't need to come racing back here at the first sign of trouble. Like I was telling her, I can take care of this myself. There's nothing she can do that I can't."

"I agree."

"Are you scaring her off?"

"It's beginning to look that way."

"What are you going to do to keep her in Chicago for the rest of the weekend?"

"I have a hunch that she might stick around one more day if she knew that those mothers and their kids had a suitable place to sleep."

Keeping his eyes on Liza Jane, he watched and waited for her reaction as he spoke to Bernice. "Take them all out to my folks' place."

Liza Jane's mouth dropped open.

CHAPTER 10

"*L*AND SAKES, MAX, I never expected you to hand over the keys to your home!" Bernice exclaimed over the phone.

"It's not my home... not anymore. Most of the rooms haven't seen the light of day since Dad died. You need to wash some sheets and take a few cleaning supplies with you."

Bernice chuckled. "I'm no stranger to hard work."

"The keys are out in the barn, on a peg by the door. Have Brodie take a claw hammer so he can pry the wood off the rest of the windows."

"Are you sure you want a houseful of strangers to come home to on Monday night?"

"I don't mind one bit, ma'am." Max glanced again at Liza Jane, who seemed to be silently fuming. "As for that other problem..."

"Elizabeth?"

"That'd be it."

"You tell her there's no reason for her to rush home now."

"I think I better leave that little job to you, if you don't mind. Somehow I doubt she'll believe me."

"Very well. Put her on."

Elizabeth hesitated before accepting the receiver from Max. She was still agitated with the way he had commandeered the phone, even if it was a gallant gesture to offer his home to the displaced women.

"I'm here, Bernice."

"And you may as well stay there, too. No sense coming home now."

"But—"

"Thanks to Maxwell, we've got some temporary housing. So you may as well wait for that pump on Monday. We still need it."

"But—"

"You weren't going to dump that job on Maxwell, were you? After making such a big to-do about going along with him?"

"I didn't exactly—"

"Like you said, he's doing us a big favor by flying up there in the first place. And now he's handing over the keys to his house. You can't very well abandon your responsibilities and hop on the next plane home."

"I... well, that is... I have responsibilities at home, too."

"Nothing that can't keep," Bernice chided gently. "I don't want to hear any more excuses. You stay in Chicago. Have a good time. Forget about us for a little while. We'll still be here when you get back Monday."

Smiling at the military command in her mother-in-law's voice, Elizabeth glanced up at Max, who looked dangerously smug. She had been outmaneuvered. Bernice had made a valid point. Elizabeth's job was to get that water pump. And she shouldn't leave it up to Max.

"It looks like I'll be seeing you on Monday night," she said with a sigh.

After Elizabeth finished her conversation with Bernice, she hung up the phone. Max was now grinning from ear to ear.

"I suppose I should be grateful for your generous offer to use your house," she said.

He dipped his head gallantly. "You're welcome."

"But I'm not thrilled with the way you brushed me aside and took over."

His charming little-boy smile beamed back at her. "White knights are like that."

"I don't want a white knight anymore, Max. I want to slay my own dragons." She watched his expression grow serious as he listened intently. "When I was sixteen, I would've given anything for you to swoop in and rescue me from my rotten relationship with my parents. But I learned to work out my problems. When I came to you for help, I didn't expect to be brushed aside *or* coddled *or* treated like I can't take care of myself."

"Is that what I've been doing?"

"To some extent," she responded with a nod. "Don't get me wrong—your help *is* appreciated. But I don't expect you or anyone else to solve my problems."

"I hear what you're saying."

She eyed him skeptically.

"Don't you believe me?" he asked defensively.

"I believe that you want to respect my wishes. I'm just not sure if you can follow through."

"Then I guess you'd better stick around to see if you're right."

Elizabeth wrestled with her own conscience. Too many times in the last twenty-four hours she had nearly succumbed to her physical attraction to Max.

"I can't stay," she finally said.

Although Max tried to understand her need to be in control, he couldn't see why she was still determined to leave. With the women and children on their way to the farmhouse, she no longer had a reason to rush back to Alton.

"What was all that talk with your mother-in- law? You said you'd see them Monday night."

"I can't stay *here*," Elizabeth corrected.

As he stepped forward, she took a hesitant step backward, causing him to stop before he reached her.

"I wish you would change your mind. You deserve to have some time to relax, to be pampered, to live in the lap of luxury for just a few short days."

"You must have me confused with someone else. I don't belong here—in a gorgeous two-bedroom suite, dressed up in a thousand-dollar sequined sheath. This isn't me. I'm the middle-class mother of two children, and we live comfortably on the insurance settlement from John's accident. Maybe not much of an income by your standards, but it pays the bills. I don't need any more than that."

Instead of retreating to the window view, she headed for a far corner of the room where a small polished table sat between two upholstered easy chairs. She stood with her back to him. He waited, watching her close herself off.

"What makes you think you don't deserve this?" He held back from crossing the room and taking her into his arms. She would only push him away, he was certain. "Talk to me, Liza Jane."

Her voice was barely above a whisper. "I don't deserve anything. Not this fancy suite. Not this beautifully elegant dress. Not the outrageously expensive dinner. And certainly not you."

He strained to hear her, uncertain if he'd heard her last words or had only imagined them.

"What's happened to you?" He cautiously approached her across the thick carpet. "You of all people deserve this chance to be happy, to start living again. Look at you. You're wasting away to nothing. What happened to that big appetite of yours? You don't eat enough to keep a bird alive. At dinner you simply pushed your food around on your plate. I swear you didn't take more than a half-dozen bites, if that."

His last comment brought a startled turn of her head. She glanced over her shoulder at him and then turned away just as quickly. "My eating habits are none of your concern."

"Yes, they are. Everything about you concerns me."

"That was a long time ago."

"Not true," he argued, standing behind her. "This is now. Johnny died in that plane crash, not you."

Tearful and angry, Elizabeth felt her pent-up emotions erupt from deep inside, exploding like a long-dormant volcano.

"John shouldn't have died any more than he should have been saddled with a wife who was still in love with his best friend!"

Her confession startled Max, leaving him no time to mask his surprise.

"I loved you so much, Max. Even when I knew you really wanted Deb, not me."

"No, it wasn't that way—"

"I knew I was your second choice. I was always afraid Deb would change her mind and you'd go back to her. Do you know how painful that was? And yet I did the same exact thing to John. I put him through the same pain, the same heartache of being second, the runner-up. I couldn't forgive myself for doing that to him. No matter how much I tried to reassure him of my love, I don't think he ever truly believed it in his heart. But he still loved me more than I deserved. I was never worthy of his love."

Max took her by the arm and turned her around.

"I want you to listen to me and listen real good." His dark eyes fixed on hers. "I'm going to tell you exactly what Johnny said about you."

Elizabeth felt a wave of panic as her gaze swept over his face. She was afraid to hear the truth, afraid of having her beliefs confirmed. "H-how would you know?"

"His mother and I had a long talk about you and Johnny... and me. Johnny told her the whole story. Everything."

"Bernice knew about us? All these years? She knew that you and I—that we...?"

His nod confirmed the unspoken question.

Elizabeth closed her eyes, mortified that her mother- in-law had known the seedier details of her past. "How can I ever look her in the face again?"

"Mrs. Mac knows we all made our share of mistakes." He quickly added, "You ought to know by now she always accepts folks just the way they are. Look at me—I gave her plenty of reason to shoo me off the back porch. I wasn't the best influence on her son. But she didn't look at me that way. She didn't judge people."

"I wish I could be more like her," Elizabeth said wistfully, her voice barely audible.

"You're a lot like her."

She disagreed but kept her opinion to herself. "What did John tell her?"

"He knew you didn't love him in the beginning. He had hoped you would learn to love him. And you did." Max paused, as if fighting with his own emotions. "He admired you for trying so hard to make the marriage work."

"We both worked hard at it."

"But he knew how guilty you felt about getting pregnant with Brodie—as if it was your entire fault and none of his. He wanted you to put the past behind you."

"I tried. That's why I wanted to be called Elizabeth. I told him it was my way of making a fresh start."

Max's gaze locked with hers. "You might be different now, but I want you to know there was nothing wrong with the girl I knew all those years ago. She just had some growing up to do. We all had some growing up to do. Even Johnny. Even me. I'm telling you the God's honest truth when I say that you deserved to be happy with Johnny."

"And I was happy." Her eyes glistened. Her voice cracked. "I really did love him, Max."

"I know that now. Johnny knew it, too. He said as much to his mom."

"He was so good to me."

"Now it's time you were good to yourself." She met his words with an awkward silence. "You give so much to everyone, but you still can't give to yourself. Why?"

"I don't know."

"You don't have to be that lost little girl looking for someone to love her."

"Was it that obvious?"

He nodded.

"I suppose I did throw myself at you."

"I don't recall that I was doing much complaining," he answered with a slight chuckle.

"Of course not." An embarrassed smile flitted over her face. "You really took on trouble when you got me."

"I think we were both feeling like a couple of unlovable misfits who happened to find each other at the right time."

"Or wrong time."

"I don't agree."

"As usual."

"You were there for me when I needed you," Max said, "even though I was too thick headed to realize it at the time. Now it's my turn to return the favor."

For a long moment he looked at her, and Elizabeth felt as if he was seeing clear through to her soul.

When he spoke again, his voice was a velvet caress. "You are the only person who needs to realize that Liza Jane has finally grown up, that the past is over."

"Yes, it *is* over—which is why I can't allow myself to get involved with you again. I've got to get on with my new life, not go backward."

"I won't deny that you have brought back a lot of memories," he admitted. "But I'm also not forgetting that we've both been traveling different roads over the years. I don't want to go back to the past, either. I want to be with you today and tomorrow and the rest of our lives. Why do you feel you don't deserve me?"

She glanced away, unable to meet his gaze. "I didn't mean for you to hear that."

He tilted his head to one side to look into her eyes. "I think you have it turned around. Maybe *I* don't deserve *you*."

"You're not a very good liar anymore," she admonished softly.

"When I wrote that letter from Germany—despite how badly I put the words on paper—I finally realized in my heart that I loved you more than anything in the world. When I lost you to Johnny, I hated myself as much as I hated the two of you. Probably more. There was a point in time when I took a good hard look at myself, and I didn't like what I saw. I didn't deserve someone like you. It kills me to admit it, but Johnny was the best damn thing that happened to you."

With a quiet catch in her voice, she said, "But why did I have to lose him before I appreciated what we had together?"

Max answered her question with one of his own. "Why did I have to lose you before I appreciated what we had together?"

She shook her head, unable to answer. The familiar ache of emptiness crept into the core of her body. She wrapped her hands around her arms and rubbed them lightly. "I feel like a hollow shell since John died. Nothing I do seems to help. I remember when food could cure anything that ailed me."

"You did have a hearty appetite, as I recall—not that I ever complained."

"Now Bernice pesters me to eat. She just can't accept that I'm not that big girl anymore. I no longer fit the image she has of me."

"She's worried about you. So am I." Max reached out for her.

As much as she wanted to be held by him, Elizabeth couldn't allow herself to give in to the temptation. He was saying all the right things to make her feel wanted and loved. But it was too late, she reminded herself. He was in love with a memory. Too much time had passed.

"The Cinderella weekend is over, Max. If you'll excuse me, I am going to shower and change clothes. Then I'll call a cab to take me to a budget motel." Avoiding his gaze, she moved toward the door to show him out. "I'll leave the designer dresses in the closet."

He followed her to the open doorway, looking positively pitiful. "If you leave now, I'll lie in bed feeling guilty as hell for letting you take off in the middle of the night."

Elizabeth refused to be baited by his sorrowful eyes. Just as she was about to turn away, he added, "The very least you could do is agree to stay until breakfast, so I can rest peacefully, knowing you're safe."

She rolled her eyes. "Oh, for heaven's sake."

"What do a few hours matter? Besides, you could use some sleep yourself. You've been up since yesterday morning. You shouldn't go out into this big city until you've rested a bit and your responses are quicker."

She was about to open her mouth to protest, but he held up his hand to stop her. "A short nap. Tiny. Minuscule. That's all I ask. Nothing more. Consider it a favor, if not for me, then for your mother-in-law." He stepped through the doorway, his hand on the doorknob. "I'll have breakfast brought up at ten and the limo waiting out front at noon. That should give you plenty of time to eat a big stack of pancakes and eggs and..."

His voice trailed off as he shut the door behind him.

"Ten? Wait a minute, Wilder. You said six-thirty earlier!" She flung the door wide. He was whistling a nondescript tune as he ambled down the hallway. "I have every intention of leaving here as soon as—"

"As soon as you eat breakfast," he called back over his shoulder. "Get some sleep."

"I'm leaving as soon as I wake up."

"Good night," he answered without looking back.

As Max returned to the second bedroom of the suite, he almost expected Liza Jane to come barreling into the hallway with her overnight bag in one hand. She was just stubborn enough to challenge his decision, a decision that he'd made in her best interest. Mrs. Mac had given him orders to take care of her daughter-in-law, and he intended to do exactly that. It was for her own good.

He stripped off his white dress shirt and tossed it over the arm of an upholstered chair, then removed his shoes and socks. An uneasy feeling crept over him as he unbuckled his belt. Something wasn't quite right.

Following his gut instinct, Max returned to the other bedroom and knocked lightly. Unable to hear any response, he slowly opened the door and heard the faint sound of the shower behind the bathroom door.

On the bed, her suitcase lay open, neatly packed and ready to go. His hunch was right—she wasn't planning to wait for breakfast. She was going to take off without telling him.

"Damn, you're a stubborn woman," he muttered, standing over the suitcase.

He rubbed his forehead, telling himself to let her go. He couldn't force her to stay. She'd made her feelings clear. No amount of arguing was going to change her mind.

Whether she would admit it or not she deserved a vacation— and more than just a couple of days. He wanted to take her on a nice, long extended trip to a warm, tropical island, where warm sun would put some color back in her cheeks. Hell, he could afford to take her whole family, if that was what was necessary to get her away from that miserable river. She needed to be rescued. And he was the only one who could do it.

He moved silently to the bathroom door, opened it a crack and peered around the edge. Through the thick mist of steam, her figure was silhouetted behind the fogged shower doors. Unaware of his presence, she stood with her back to him, washing her hair. When she shifted her stance, he felt his blood thicken. He imagined the heated sensation of joining their bodies under the warm spray of water. He imagined her closing her eyes and letting herself surrender to the fire between them. He wanted to make the fantasy come true, to feel her make love to him with rekindled passion.

Not yet. He had promised to wait for her to come to him and he would keep his promise.

Seeing a neat stack of clean clothes within easy reach, he snatched them and snuck out of the bathroom. Though her bag had been packed, he checked the drawers and closet for anything she might be able to wear. Certain she didn't have any clothes left for her, he dumped the pile into the suitcase and attempted to close it. No luck. He picked it up while bits of fabric poked out of all sides.

Out of the corner of his eye, he glimpsed her purse on the bedside table. Her credit card could easily ruin his scheme.

The shower stopped.

Awkwardly shifting the overflowing suitcase, he freed one hand to grab her purse, then silently slipped out of her room. Striding barefoot down the carpeted hall, he felt a twinge of guilt for stealing all her belongings. Well, not actually stealing. Borrowing. Only for a few hours. She needed to rest. Afterward, he would return her things and she could be on her way with his blessing.

CHAPTER 11

$\mathcal{M}$AX DEPOSITED THE OVERLOADED BAG on the floor of his closet and headed toward the bed. Leaving the last of his clothes in a pile on the floor, he had just climbed into bed—and heard her frustrated wail.

"Max...!"

"Have a nice nap, Liza Jane," he murmured with a grin, punching the pillow in the center. Exhausted beyond belief, he wondered how he would ever catch up on all the hours of sleep he had missed over the last several weeks. As he settled his head into the soft contours of the pillow, he thought of nestling his body against the soft contours of the woman in the next room.

Renewed desire flared in his groin, hardening him to the point of discomfort. His mind raced back to her slender silhouette in the shower and his breathing quickened. Trying to block the images, he rolled to his side, only to feel the cotton sheet brush against his arousal. He groaned and threw back the bed covers. The only remedy was a cold shower. Ice-cold.

He swung his legs over the side and sat on the edge of the bed, gripping the corner of the mattress. He could feel the sweet agony tensing every muscle in his body. No other woman but

Liza Jane had this kind of effect on him. He had a few relationships that had lasted long enough for him to hope that love would grow deeper with time. It never had.

Any romantic notions about love and passion had long since died, buried with his Wildman days, left behind in Alton. He had been naive enough to think he could come back to his hometown for a few short weeks without digging up old feelings. Liza Jane had become nothing more than a ghost of the past, a hauntingly beautiful memory. Or so he thought.

He never imagined running into her, let alone feeling anything but indifference toward her. What a fool he'd been.

And he was a bigger fool for thinking that one weekend alone with her would change everything. He shouldn't have tried to recapture the past. He was not thinking rationally—or at least not with the upper part of his anatomy.

Max levered himself off the bed, disgusted with his inability to control his own body. Liza Jane was driving him crazy without doing a single thing to seduce him. Yet he was as seduced by her as any man could be.

~

ELIZABETH HAD HUNTED for her clothes in every corner of her hotel room. The more she looked, the angrier she became. Convinced that Max was the thief, she wrapped the large bath towel tighter around her body and marched down the hall.

Throwing open his door, she demanded, "Hand over my clothes, Wilder."

Seeing his magnificent nude body completely disarmed her anger. The sight of his sculpted muscles sent a quiver down her spine. His arousal sent a quiver into the feminine depth of her body.

She clutched the edge of the towel above her breasts, battling the desire to release it and go to him. Her legs felt weak, incapable of moving her across the room. Yet, had he taken the first step, she knew she couldn't turn away from his dark gaze.

Make love to me, Max. Please. Before I lose my nerve, before I run away from you.

She glanced at the bed, remembering hot, sultry afternoons when their sweat-sheened bodies had writhed together in glorious ecstasy. Every time she'd reached the zenith of pleasure, she'd felt as though she had died a little in his arms. Would it be that way again? How she wanted to find out. How she wanted to feel those agonizingly sweet moments again.

You didn't feel those things with John.

Yes, I did! He was my husband! I loved him!

But he never made love to you the way Max did.

No! Stop this! I don't want to think...

The startling thoughts jerked her to her senses. Staring at the empty mattress, she inched backward out of the room. "I—I'm sorry, John."

"John?"

Her head snapped up. "Max... I said *Max*."

"No, you didn't, Liza Jane."

"Elizabeth," she snapped. "I'm not Liza Jane anymore. She's dead and buried."

"Just like your husband?"

"Y-yes."

"Then what made you call me *John*?" Max stepped closer, unconcerned about his nudity. She didn't move. "Johnny is as much a presence in this room as I am. Maybe more."

She shook her head. "No, he's gone."

"Tell me something," Max said, as one finger trailed over the back of her hand. "If I made love to you right now, would you be thinking of Johnny?"

"That's not a fair question."

"It isn't?"

He hooked the top of her towel with one finger. She relaxed

her grip on the soft white terry cloth. As he closed the space between them, she leaned away until the corner of the wooden door frame pressed between her shoulder blades. She held her breath. He bent his head to kiss her neck and his own warm breath against her skin sent a ripple of desire through her.

"Me or Johnny?" he repeated in a husky whisper.

"Don't..."

His head came up slowly. She stared at his lips, wishing he would stop asking her questions she couldn't answer, wouldn't answer. Her gaze drifted up to his face and found his dark blue eyes watching, waiting.

"I—I can't do this, Max." Her voice was a hoarse whisper. "I thought that I wanted it..." *And I do! God help me, I do!* "But you were right about John. Even though sometimes it feels like it has been twenty years instead of two since I lost him, there are days when I feel like it was yesterday. I still catch myself talking to him, expecting him to answer from the next room. He's still with me. I'm sorry."

She placed her palms against Max's bare chest and gently pushed him away. When he stepped back, she was relieved that he was allowing her to leave without another word.

"Earlier, you said that you'd made a promise. Was it to Johnny?"

"No." Why did he have to bring that up now? She had hoped that her slip had gone unnoticed. She should have known better than to expect Max to ignore it. "I didn't make a promise to John. Or to Bernice, for that matter."

"What was the promise?"

"I'd rather not say." As she moved into the hall, he reached out and lightly grasped her arm.

"Please tell me, Elizabeth."

A simple touch should not have felt like a powerful magnet drawing her into his arms. She closed her eyes and tilted her head back, pleading with herself to keep the tears locked away.

She couldn't let him see how easily he could reach the deepest part of her with merely a touch.

Maybe it was time he knew. Maybe if she told him of her solemn vow...

She opened her eyes to look at him. "When I found out I was pregnant, I didn't want to marry John. I still wanted you, even if I was your second choice. So I planned to claim the baby was yours. It could have been. It *should* have been. I was going to use my pregnancy to get you to marry me."

"What stopped you?"

His question drew her back to the day she had visited the health clinic in Saint Louis. Learning about her pregnancy left her numb with shock. She drove home, locked herself in her room and cried herself to sleep. She had a nightmare of Max refusing to acknowledge the baby as his and turning his back on her. She woke up sobbing, realizing she couldn't go through with the deception.

Alone and frightened, Elizabeth had made a solemn vow to herself. If John married her, she would do everything in her power to be a good wife and mother. She vowed to give up Max and never look back.

Elizabeth blinked, dragging her thoughts back to the present, bringing the room into focus. Standing before her was the one man she couldn't have.

"I had to make a sacrifice if I was going to have a father for my son."

"I was the sacrificial lamb?"

She winced at his tone of sarcasm, then slowly nodded. "I know it may sound ridiculous to you."

"The way I figure it, whatever deal you made with yourself was canceled when Johnny died in that plane crash. As for this sacrificial lamb—I'm back and I'm staying."

"Don't make fun of this, Max."

"Do I look like I'm laughing?" His gaze held her captive for a long moment before she shook her head. As he released his hold on her arm, the warmth of his touch lingered. The agonizing decision hung in the air between them. Her body trembled with the longing to join their flesh. But her mind was a jumble of doubt and guilt.

His questioning gaze demanded an answer.

"I can't," she said, then saw the hurt in his eyes. "Not yet."

His expression brightened. He dropped a quick kiss on her lips. "Then there's still hope."

"About my clothes—"

"Consider them ransom. Your clothes will be returned after you've gotten some sleep and eaten a decent breakfast."

"You're incorrigible."

He winked. "And you love it."

"At least offer me something to sleep in."

"My bed?"

"My nightgown!"

"Well, I tried."

"Some things never change."

~

AN HOUR LATER, Elizabeth still lay awake, staring into the blackness of her hotel bedroom. Her mind refused to acknowledge the need for sleep, insisting upon arguing with itself, filling her head with conflicting thoughts.

Thoughts of Max. She didn't want to be thinking of him lying naked in the next room. She didn't want to be feeling the tension in her body, which seemed to escalate with every intake of breath. Her promise haunted her. Going back on her vow seemed like a betrayal to John.

You deserve to be happy.

The words were so clear she almost believed Max had entered the room and whispered them in her ear. Her body responded to the fantasy with a tingling sensation that began at her earlobe and rippled down over her flesh, setting her skin on fire.

"I can't do this," she said firmly under her breath, curling up on her side. She pressed her knees together, trying to stop the ache.

Johnny's gone. His death released you from your vow.

She felt her resolve slip with each pounding beat of her heart.

Go to Max.

"No!"

You need him.

"No!"

He needs *you.*

Denial died in her throat. Her palms itched, a sensation of tiny pinpricks. It was her body's own quirky way of nudging her to face her fears, even if they scared the daylights out of her. She rubbed her hands together, then squeezed her eyes shut.

"Just for tonight... That's all," she murmured.

She would prove to Max that this sexual attraction between them wasn't really love. Then they could both go on with their separate lives and stop looking back on what could have been.

Elizabeth felt clumsy and awkward as she made her way down the darkened hall and fumbled with the doorknob to Max's room. The sound of his slow, slumbering breaths guided her to the edge of his bed.

Would he think this was a dream? She struggled with the tiny pearl buttons of her summer nightgown, not sure the entire weekend wasn't a dream while she slept at home in her bed. Maybe that was why it was easier to come to him now. She could pretend it was all a part of an elaborate fantasy. Yes, the weekend in Chicago. The fancy hotel. The elegant dinner. The romantic evening. None of it felt real.

Leaving her gown on the floor, she slipped beneath the covers and moved to his side, finding him on his back in the center of the bed, the sheet across his bare midriff and one arm slung above his head. She reached out a trembling hand and rested it lightly on his broad chest. Short, soft curls prickled her palm, and made her recall the sensation she'd experienced earlier. An odd quiver went through her that she couldn't quite define. Fear? Anticipation? Then it was gone as quickly as it came.

Her hand rose and fell with his deep, rhythmic breathing. As her light caress traveled downward, she felt a searing heat in the pit of her belly. She drew her fingertips over his hip and down his thigh, purposefully avoiding, purposefully titillating. His breathing quickened. She paused, startled, but despite his low groan, he was still asleep. She relaxed.

Her fingertips slid to the inside of his knee, then slowly upward. She gently cupped the soft spheres, eliciting his moan of pleasure.

~

MAX DRIFTED IN A GLORIOUS dream world. He was flying his Beech-17 over the flooded Mississippi, with Liza Jane next to him. Her perfume pulled his attention from the skies as her hand moved over him and dipped between his thighs. She had made the first move. She had come to him.

Finally.

His mind swirled with a collage of blue skies and white clouds, instrument lights and the face of an angel. The drone of the plane engine echoed in his ears as he groaned and twisted toward Liza Jane, wanting to lift her onto his lap. He would make love to her right there in the pilot's seat. It was crazy. It was reckless. It was impossible. But as the pressure built deep within his loins, he knew nothing could stop him from having her.

She seemed to sense the direction of his thoughts, slipping one leg over his thighs. His hands bracketed her narrow hips. She felt so fragile and small. He didn't want to hurt her. With only the most extreme self-control, he held back his own hunger and let her take the initiative.

In one swift, penetrating movement, she sheathed him to the base of his thick, hardened shaft. Intense pleasure ripped through him as her gasp of ecstasy reached his ears. The sound wakened him.

His eyes flew open.

Max could barely see Liza Jane in the night-shrouded room. But he could feel her. He could feel the tight, moist heat of her inner core. His fingers curled into the soft flesh of her thighs, straddling his hips.

He whispered in a hoarse rasp, "Liza Jane? What the—"

Her fingertips touched his lips, silencing him. She didn't speak, didn't make a sound, as her feminine walls tightened around his manhood, then released. Tightened. Released. With her own rhythm, she moved up and down, slick and ready for him.

Torn between confusion and sweet agony, he gripped her slender arms. "Liza Jane," he repeated, his voice raw and husky. "Hold on a second."

Her mouth dropped to his, kissing him with the same deep, erotic penetration. Her hips kept rocking against him, building the pressure.

His mind battled with his body. He wanted nothing more than to grip her tight little bottom and let her ride him over the top to oblivion.

But his damn pride kept bringing him back to their argument. What the hell had changed her mind? What had possessed her to come creeping back into his room under the cloak of darkness? What about her promise? What about Johnny?

An uneasy feeling sneaked up on him, warring with the escalation of passion. With tongues intertwined, he wrapped his arms around her and rolled her onto her back. Her thighs locked around his hips. Unable to rein in his carnal desire, he thrust deeply into her. She cried out, arching her spine.

In the darkness, he gazed down upon her face, stunned to see two glistening trails of tears. Was it pain or pleasure that caused her tortured expression?

"Liza Jane?" He stopped all movement.

Her shuttered eyes opened wide, searching his face. Only their ragged breathing could be heard in the silent room. He opened his mouth to speak, but she shook her head vigorously.

"Don't talk," she pleaded, a catch in her voice. "Make love to me. Let me pretend for a little while."

She laced her fingers behind his neck and pulled his mouth down to hers. The kiss held a promise of passion, yet he sensed a desperation so great that he longed to wrap his body around her in a protective cocoon so he could keep her safe forever.

Let me just pretend for a little while. Pretend what?

The vague, uneasy feeling suddenly became a brawny fist that slammed into the center of his chest. Hadn't she called him John earlier? Was she thinking of Johnny now, instead of him? The questions led him to only one conclusion. She snuck into his room in the dead of night so she wouldn't see the face of her lover in the dark. She didn't want him to talk, to spoil the illusion. She wanted to pretend he was Johnny.

Her hips moved against him. He couldn't stop his body from betraying his desire. He cursed the need she created in him. He cursed Johnny for being everything he wasn't. Liza Jane had come to his bed, hoping the darkness would trick her mind into believing he was her beloved Johnny.

Max wanted to damn her for using him this way. But he couldn't bring himself to hate her for having a broken heart. He couldn't condemn her for wanting the one person she had loved... and lost. He remembered the same pain and loneliness. And damned if he hadn't ended up in bed with one woman after another, hoping to find someone who could make him feel the way Liza Jane had. None of them ever did. But that didn't stop him from breaking a lot of hearts along the way.

Even though his own heart ached, he would give her what she asked. He would remain silent. He would hold her. He would make love to her. And he would pretend he was her husband. If that's what she wanted, that's what she would get.

CHAPTER 12

*E*LIZABETH ENDURED A LONG MOMENT of escalating apprehension as Max seemed to wrestle with his own thoughts. Just as she was about to abandon her blatant seduction and apologize for humiliating herself, Max brought his mouth down to hers and kissed her gently. Slowly he withdrew from her body, then slid his hand over her belly to the tantalizing nub of her womanhood. Each caress created wave upon wave of ecstasy. With shortened breaths, she rode the crest of the highest swell. His intimate massage continued, taking her once again beyond the reaches of her mind and body. On the third crescendo, his hands slipped beneath her bottom and tilted her so he entered her smoothly and swiftly. She met each thrust, taking him deeper inside her body.

His muscles tensed. His pelvis rocked. His breath escaped his lungs in bestial grunts of pleasure. His animalistic passion unleashed her own primal response, so long locked away. She clung to him, her fingers kneading the muscled flesh of his long back. Her legs pulled him in. He buried his face in her neck, muffling a guttural scream of release that sent a quiver down her spine.

Nothing had prepared her for the impact of this moment. The power of his body inside her, outside her, all around her, was beyond anything they had shared ages ago as carelessly wild teenagers. Overwhelmed with awe and contentment, Elizabeth lay beneath him, listening to their panting breaths. He inhaled deeply, his chest expanding, pressing the air from her lungs until she gave a tiny squeak of distress.

He lifted his head from her shoulder, propping himself on his elbows. "I'm too heavy," he said apologetically, and began to shift his weight off her.

She shook her head, tightening her arms and legs around him, keeping him inside her just a little while longer. With a smile on her lips, she closed her eyes and lightly skimmed her fingernails along his back. His moan of pleasure rumbled through his chest like the purr of a big, contented jungle cat.

Lord, how wonderful it felt to be thoroughly sated and completely spent. Every fiber of her being was exhausted, yet alert and awake. She could almost hear her muscles humming with the same energy of high-voltage power lines, sending an involuntary shiver down her limbs.

"Cold?" he asked, then nibbled on her earlobe.

"No... hot." She turned her head slightly and kissed him. As their lips parted, she lightly tightened her thighs. Inside her feminine recesses, her muscles contracted around his manhood.

"How in the hell do you do that?" His husky voice held a tone of awe.

With a short chuckle, she traced her tongue along his lower lip. The effect of her rhythmic movements quickly restored his virile strength, until he filled her once more.

Amazed and aroused, Max murmured naughty little things in her ear that would have made her blush during the light of day. Instead, they made her feel decadent and sexy and capable of driving him mad in her arms.

~

A THIN RAY OF SUNLIGHT peered through the crack in the drapes as Max slowly awakened with Liza Jane slumbering in his arms, her back pressed against his chest. His cloudy vision focused on the digital numbers of the bedside clock. Ten-thirty. Two hours of sleep had not lessened his exhaustion, but he wasn't complaining. They had made love throughout the early-morning hours, each time better than the last. Now that the hour had come for her to leave, he couldn't bring himself to wake her. Not yet.

His left arm draped over her hip. His fingers intertwined with hers. Her slow, even breathing was soothing to his ears. This is what he wanted to wake up to every day. Holding her. Loving her.

As he unlaced his fingers from hers and splayed his hand against her flat abdomen, he found it hard to imagine that a baby had once grown in there, especially a big boy like Brodie. The son that could have been his own. *Should* have been.

A wave of jealousy washed over him as he thought of his best friend with Liza Jane, touching her, impregnating her in a moment of compassion. One time together and all their lives had changed.

What were the odds that it could happen again? Astronomical, of course. But so were the odds of winning the lottery. He smiled to himself. He had already beaten the odds once. Maybe luck was still on his side.

One time was all it took, he reminded himself. His palm felt the heat of her body. What if she was wrong about her female problems? What if their night together had gotten her pregnant? The possibility thrilled him.

She would marry him for sure. She'd have to. He was certain she wouldn't consider any other choice. She loved being a mother. He recalled the way her eyes got all misty when she talked about her two kids. He remembered the scene in the kitchen at the boardinghouse, when she'd held the sleeping toddler in her arms. She loved children. She loved babies. Why wouldn't she welcome another child of her own?

It was exactly what she needed. What they *both* needed, Max realized. He had never given any thought to having his own family, not until he had suspected Brodie of being his own flesh and blood.

Lying on his side, Max relished the feel of her slender body molded to his own, her soft bottom pressed against his stomach. He smiled at the memory of seeing the tiny rose tattoo, surprised yet pleased that it was still there. Over the years, he had considered having his own tattoo removed because it brought back too many memories. Did she feel the same way?

His fingertips traced her rib cage. Her thin figure suited the fashion magazines, but he wondered if losing so much weight was an indication of something seriously wrong that would affect the health of a baby.

His initial euphoria waned. He was kidding himself. Liza Jane was wasting away, grieving for her dead husband. It was Johnny she really wanted, not him.

She stirred in his arms, stretching slightly, arching her back. In her sleepy state, she wasn't aware her bottom pressed against his groin. His body responded, primed and ready.

Another chance to get her pregnant? Another chance to play Johnny?

She shifted onto her back. There was enough light in the dim room for her to see him for who he was—Max, not Johnny. When he made love to her this time, she couldn't pretend she was in the arms of her husband.

He gazed down into green eyes that studied him, uncertain and wary. He recognized that look of regret. He had been there plenty of times in his life, waking up with a lovely young woman in his bed. Regret always crept in with the morning glare of reality.

Elizabeth watched Max watching her. A lock of dark hair fell across his forehead as he stared down at her with questions in his eyes. What had last night meant? Where did they go from here? She didn't know, but she wasn't ready for it to end just yet. She had found heaven in his arms, beyond anything she could have dreamed. Although an inner voice chided her for enjoying it so much, another part of her ignored the guilty conscience.

She reached up and combed her fingers through his tousled hair.

He turned his face and reverently kissed the inside of her forearm, sending a tingle through her body.

Turning his gaze back to her, he asked, "Can we talk about last night?"

"I'd rather not." A feeling of dread swept over her. She couldn't promise him anything. "Please try to understand..."

A muscle along his jaw twitched. "What exactly am I supposed to understand? Do you want to forget last night ever happened?"

She shook her head. "No."

"But you aren't exactly proud of yourself this morning, am I right?"

"Wrong."

"Then why am I seeing regret written all over your face?"

"Maybe you're looking a little too hard to find something that isn't there."

She knew the signs of a fight brewing between them, but she refused to play along. Instead, she quickly moved to the opposite side of the bed. With her back to him, she sat on the edge of the mattress, grabbed her nightgown off the floor and slipped it over her head before she switched on the bedside lamp.

Without turning around, she took a deep breath to steady her nerves and let it out slowly. "I need a cup of coffee. Do you mind if I order some?"

"Go right ahead," he said curtly. "Have some breakfast delivered, too, while you're at it."

"What do you want?" The tension between them remained as taut as a circus high-wire. She saw herself balancing precariously in the middle with no net—Johnny on the platform behind her, Max on the one in front of her.

"I'll have whatever you're having."

"I'm not hungry."

He muttered an oath under his breath. The bed jiggled as he moved behind her. She risked a glance over her shoulder. He rolled over and reached for the bedside phone, ordering a quantity of food that would feed the entire group of women and children at the shelter. As he cradled the receiver, she rose to her feet.

"You're not too good at this," he observed.

Surprised by his candid remark, she wasn't certain if she'd heard him correctly. She turned to see him reclined on the pillows in a deliciously sexy pose, the sheet riding low on his hips.

"I beg your pardon? I'm not too good?"

"Don't get your feathers ruffled all over again. I wasn't talking about sex." He paused, a grin spreading over his face. "*That* goes without saying."

"Glad you approved."

He laughed. A tentative smile crept to the corners of her mouth. "Now that's what I want to see—a smile on your face. Relax. It's not all that hard."

"What?"

"The morning after."

"Am I so easy to read?"

"Let's just say I've been there."

"I haven't. Not even once." She gazed at him lying in the bed they had shared and realized she had never spent the entire night with Max, never seen him like this in the morning. Their teenage love affair hadn't allowed for luxury hotel rooms and long romantic weekends. Hot, passionate lovemaking took place at the drive-in and in haylofts, in a field of wildflowers and on remote country roads. Every night when they kissed goodbye in front of her house, she had wished for the day she could wake up in his arms, happily married to him, living together with a houseful of children.

He patted the mattress next to him. "Come here." When she hesitated, he added, "I won't bite."

"I know."

"Then lie down beside me. On top of the blankets, if you want."

"You must think I'm crazy."

"Not at all," he answered with a slight shake of his head. He held his arm up as she lowered herself next to him, then draped it over her shoulder. "Actually, I think you're adorable. I like the fact that you're not exactly an expert in this area."

"But you are."

"Ancient history."

"How ancient?" His silence prompted her to look up at him. His dark eyebrows pulled together. He lifted her hand to his lips and kissed the back of it "Max...?"

"I sowed some wild oats for a few years. There was even a time when I settled down for a while."

"You had a wife?" She felt a strange and surprising twinge of jealousy.

"No. Neither of us wanted marriage."

"How long were you together?"

He hesitated, as if weighing his decision to answer or not. "Seven years."

Elizabeth was speechless. Seven years was a lot longer than a simple relationship. He may as well have been married.

"Quit staring at me like I've got two heads." He chuckled, gently pressing her head back down to his shoulder.

"Do you still see her?"

"No, not at all. We went our separate ways five or six years ago."

"Do you still have feelings for her?"

He pondered her question. "A part of me still cares about her, still thinks of her from time to time and hopes that she's found a happy life."

The same thoughts about Max had crossed her mind over the years, yet she would never admit it. "Do you think she did?"

"Yep, I'm sure she did."

"How can you be so certain if you haven't seen her?"

"She believed that we each create our own happiness. Not through other people. Not through outside circumstances."

"Somehow I can't picture you with a female philosopher. Was she a therapist?"

"No. Just a free spirit. Intelligent. Creative. In charge of animation development with a major film studio."

Elizabeth let out a soft whistle of amazement. "And you didn't want to marry her?"

"We were too good of friends."

"But that makes for a better marriage."

"Not necessarily. Good sex makes a good marriage."

"Not necessarily." Her mimicked response came out of her mouth too quickly to stop it. "That is... I mean... A real relationship is not only about sexual compatibility."

"Not in my book."

"I bet your book also has centerfolds."

"Diagrams," he corrected. "Anatomically correct, scientific diagrams."

"Road maps of the human anatomy?"

"Something like that."

"Real men don't need road maps.".

"Ha-ha."

"They never stop and ask for directions, either."

"Of course not. We rely on natural instinct."

"Are you saying that as a *real man* you have no need for centerfolds?"

Max slid down beside her until they were face-to- face, nose-to-nose. A twinkle of mischief lit his blue eyes.

"I've pretty much got all the roads memorized—" His right hand traveled down her nightgown, skimming over her belly and dipping between her legs. "—especially some particularly breath-taking points of interest. What do you think?"

With a deep intake of breath, she slowly nodded. "You're good, I'll give you that."

"Good?" His hand stilled as his head drew back and he eyed her with feigned hurt. "Just *good?*"

"Okay. Great."

"Not excellent? Fantastic? Out of this world?"

As if responding to a lesson in elementary school, she play-fully recited after him, "You're excellent... Fantastic... Out of this world."

Instead of a smug response, he grew serious, his voice soft-ened. "So are you."

She touched his cheek with her fingertips, her smile barely moving the corners of her mouth. "This *is* wonderful and I don't want it to end but—"

"Then don't let it end."

"The only thing we've established in the last several hours is that we are still physically compatible in bed."

"Is this a reference from *your* book?"

She ignored his remark. "I'm not saying I don't love what you do to me."

"Then you are saying you don't love *me*."

Cupping his face with her hands, she swallowed hard to dislodge the sudden knot in her throat. "How can I say I love you when...?"

"When you still love Johnny?"

Forcing back the tears, she simply nodded. Max's pain-filled eyes closed for the space of several heartbeats. When he opened them, he met her gaze. "Do you ever think there will be a chance... that you—"

She laid her fingertips against his lips. "It's too soon, Max."

He kissed the pads of her fingers and smiled a halfhearted smile. "Thank you."

Had he misunderstood her? "I didn't say yes."

"You didn't say no, either," he answered, drawing her into his arms.

~

BY THE TIME MAX FINISHED his breakfast, it was nearly noon. Sitting across the glass-topped table from him, Elizabeth sipped her second cup of coffee. Her pancakes remained untouched on the plate in front of her. She had eaten the orange slices and one piece of plain, dry toast.

"Are you going to eat your bacon?" he asked, nodding at it.

"If I don't, do I still get my clothes back?"

He seemed puzzled until her question jogged his memory, then he laughed. "A deal's a deal."

"Fine." She picked up the bacon as if it were an insect.

"Give it to me."

"And let you keep my clothes for the entire weekend? I don't think so."

"I'll give you back your things. Now hand over the damn plate."

She gave him the rest of her breakfast. "You have quite an appetite."

"Not usually." He winked, taking her dish and setting it down on his own. "I worked hard last night, thanks to you."

"*You* worked hard, thanks to *me*?"

He waved his fork back and forth. "Correction—I worked hard last night *and loved every second of it*, thanks to you."

She grinned. "That sounds much better."

"I'm surprised you're not hungry."

"I've got a bit of a queasy stomach."

A crisp slice of bacon was an inch from his mouth as he paused, gazing slack-jawed at her. "Morning sickness?"

"Boy, you really don't know about babies, do you?" She smiled like a mother to her child. "It's way too early to have morning sickness. That is, *if* I were pregnant, which I'm *not*."

"You're sure."

"It would take a miracle." She took another sip of coffee.

"Stranger things have been known to happen."

Lowering her cup to its saucer, she sighed. "Caffeine probably isn't helping my stomach, either. But it keeps me going."

"Have you ever tried eating food? I've heard it works wonders." His congenial sarcasm brought a small smile to her lips.

"I'll keep it in mind."

As she began to raise her cup, he leaned forward and wrapped his hand around her wrist. "*Will* you keep it in mind?" he asked, all levity gone.

"We were joking around, Max."

"I'm not." He released her arm and sat back in his chair. "Let's say you *did* get pregnant last night. Aren't you concerned about the health of a baby?"

She stiffened. "I would never jeopardize the health of my child."

"Then why jeopardize your own?"

"It's not intentional, I assure you."

"Okay, then eat this." Offering her own plate back to her, he said gently, "Prove it to me."

Her gaze bounced to the food, then back to him, green eyes clouded with nervous apprehension. "This is ridiculous."

"Humor me."

With a tight chuckle, she reached out for her breakfast. "Even though I'm perfectly capable of eating it all, I'm not about to finish this entire meal when I'm not hungry."

"Four pancakes."

"Two."

"Three. Plus one of the eggs."

"They're cold."

"Three plus—"

She cut him off. "Two pancakes and a little fruit."

Max nodded, then watched her attack the food with a vengeance, her fork clicking against the ceramic plate. In her dramatic enthusiasm, she oohed and aahed over the taste of the fresh creamery butter, sweet maple syrup, succulent strawberries and mouthwatering melon balls. Despite her convincing performance, she ate only the amount she agreed to eat.

"How do you feel now?" he asked when she finished.

Her smile was overly bright. "Excellent! Fantastic! Out of this world!"

His narrowed gaze didn't disturb her in the least. She lifted her napkin from her lap and neatly placed it on the table beside her dirty dishes.

Smug triumph was written on her face. The time had come for him to relinquish her clothes.

CHAPTER 13

*M*AX PUSHED HIS CHAIR BACK with reluctance. "I'll be right back."

As he retrieved the suitcase from the back of the closet, he recalled his suggestion of morning sickness to Liza Jane, wishing now that he had kept his thoughts to himself. Hoping to get her pregnant was a damn-fool's fantasy. Competing with the ghost of her husband was pushing him beyond rational thinking.

He shook his head in disgust with himself. Maybe she would be better off without him. His presence was only bringing back too many painful memories. Maybe it was time to let her go.

He walked back to the living room with her open suitcase, the contents spilling out the sides. Standing silently at the entrance, he gazed at her across the room. She was still sitting at the dining table, her back to him. Her dark blond hair fell loose and soft over her shoulders.

He longed to touch her again, to coax her into his bed again, to beg her to stay. A tightness inside his chest climbed into his throat. The back of his eyes stung. He had to face the truth. She wanted Johnny, not him.

"I'll put these in your room," he said, only after regaining some control of his vocal cords. "How soon should I tell the limo driver to be here?"

She pivoted in her chair, her hand on her stomach. Her face was pale. "I don't think I'm quite up to leaving just yet."

Max dropped the overstuffed luggage on the couch and rushed to her side. Kneeling at her feet, he smoothed her hair away from her cheek. "You're not hot. Do you feel hot? I don't think you have a fever."

"But I don't think those pancakes did my stomach a favor."

"Oh."

"Yeah, oh," she repeated dully. "You always could goad me into doing something foolish. But I thought by now I'd have learned a thing or two about following my own gut instinct."

Discomfort etched on her face, she inhaled deeply through her nose and blew air out in a slow, concentrated effort. Max mentally kicked himself for bullying her into eating breakfast. "Maybe you should lie down."

"Only for a little while. I need to call home first."

"I'll call after I put you to bed."

When he started to lift her in his arms, she protested. "I'd rather walk."

"And I'd rather carry you." He scooped her off the chair and headed toward her room. "It's the least I can do after forcing you to eat too much."

"What's this? Is Wildman feeling guilty?"

"Extremely."

"Good."

With her arms looped around his neck, he gazed down at her upturned face. Her attempt to lighten the moment couldn't keep him from noticing the darkened shadows beneath her tired eyes.

After he lowered her onto her unmade bed, she curled on her left side, her fist pressed into her midsection. Max covered her with the blankets and sat down on the edge of the mattress next to her.

Smoothing his hand over her hair, he asked, "Do you want me to call the concierge to have some stomach medicine brought up?"

"Don't say *brought up*," she groaned, shaking her head against the pillow. He picked up the phone, but her hand slipped out from beneath the sheet and touched his knee. "No medicine. I'll be okay in a bit. Would you call Bernice, though?"

"Of course." He called her house, the boarding house and his own farmhouse before he tracked down Bernice. When the woman learned that her daughter-in-law had not left Chicago, she sounded relieved.

"No sense in ruining a perfectly wonderful weekend by rushing home for no good reason."

Max gazed down at Liza Jane as her eyelids closed tightly, then flew open. Wordlessly, she shoved him off the bed and sprinted for the bathroom, one hand cupped over her mouth.

In the flurry of commotion, he heard Bernice say that the mothers and children were settling in nicely at his farmhouse, then thanked him again. He mindlessly murmured a response, his attention focused on the closed bathroom door.

"I knew I could count on you to talk Elizabeth out of coming home."

"I didn't talk her out of anything."

"What did you do?"

He blew out a long breath before he answered her with guilty resignation. "I made her sick."

~

ELIZABETH HAD BEEN SOAKING in a warm bubble bath for forty-five minutes when Max knocked at her door for his ten-minute update on her safety.

"I haven't drowned yet," she called out, feeling so much more like herself. Thankfully, her nausea was gone.

"Didn't mean to disturb you."

"Yes, you did."

"Excuse me for being concerned," he answered lightly.

"You're excused."

Though he didn't respond, she sensed his presence on the other side of the door. She ignored the temptation to invite him in. "I said you're excused."

"I'll be back."

She smiled, charmed by his attentiveness throughout the entire day. After she had slept enough to take the edge off her exhaustion, she had awakened alone in her bed, the scent of roses filling the air. While she was sleeping, he had ordered several floral arrangements and placed them around the spacious room.

With some rest and a small cup of vegetable soup, she was feeling much better. Refusing to dwell on her indelicate scene after breakfast, she got out of the tub and toweled off.

Her image in the mirror drew her attention. The reflection was strange and unfamiliar. She had a pear-shaped body, with long, thin arms and legs that had little muscle tone. Her breasts no longer filled the B-cup bras bought after throwing out the larger sizes last year.

What did Max find so attractive? She turned left and right in her scrupulous inspection. The petite red rose on her derriere brought back a sweet memory of him touching it with tender reverence. For the first time in years, she looked at the tattoo without regret and shame. Tucking away this special memory, she found her thoughts wandering back to the self-analysis of all her physical flaws.

Despite her weight loss, her body didn't look like what she had expected. Sure, she finally had a flat stomach, but it was marked with fine, silvery lines. She ran a fingertip along the faint stretch mark, remembering Max's concern about a baby. She felt a flutter in her stomach at the idea of having another child growing in her. Her eyes misted with sentimental yearning.

It was sheer nonsense to contemplate a future of maternity smocks and diapers and two a.m. feedings. Her nipples puckered. Her breasts tingled.

From the cold air-conditioning, she told herself, wrapping her body tightly in the terry robe even as images lingered in her mind—images of nursing a tiny infant, of Max sitting next to her and stroking the downy hair of their newborn.

No! She cinched the robe's belt with a hard yank. *It won't happen. It will never happen.*

Brodie and Annie were the only children she would have. The doctors had confirmed it years ago. Her recently interrupted cycles were more of a blessing than a curse. She didn't need the monthly inconvenience, especially now that she had chosen to be intimate with a man.

Not just any man. Max. After all these years he wanted her back. Why? She couldn't give him the children he could have with another woman. From the way he had been intent on claiming Brodie as his son, she knew he wanted his own flesh and blood walking the face of the earth, carrying his family genes into the next generation.

In the middle of taking down her hair, she paused, bobby pins in her hand. Her freshly washed face stared back at her in the mirror. Her eyelids drooped too much. Her nose was too bulbous. Were those new freckles across her cheek or were they called age spots after thirty? She was thirty-six, not sixteen anymore. The Rubenesque body that had been an embarrassment was now the slender but sagging figure of a grieving widow.

"Some catch," she muttered, dropping the pins in the tray on the counter and reaching for her brush.

"Did you call me?"

She couldn't stop the smile even if she wanted to. "Has it been ten minutes already?"

"No, but..." Max stopped when he heard the snick of the latch on the bathroom door.

"You can come in," she announced from the other side. He gently pushed the door open.

"You're dressed."

"Close enough. Sorry to disappoint you."

He lifted the brush from her hand and took over the task, grinning at her astonished expression reflected in the mirror. Damp tendrils of hair framed the perfect shape of her face. The warmth of the bath had left her skin looking delicate and luminescent. But it was those jade-green eyes that captured him, mesmerized him. He could never tire of gazing at her.

"I wish I could take a picture of you," he said, slowly drawing the bristles through her thick blond hair.

Puzzled, she asked, "Like this?"

"Exactly like this." He chuckled at her skepticism, stroking the brush downward again. "No makeup. Just you."

"I look rather... plain."

"Where did you come up with *that* idea?"

She shrugged. "Once an ugly duckling, always an ugly duckling."

Even though he was tempted to toss away the brush and kiss some sense into her, he forced his hand to continue its leisurely brush strokes. "But the ugly duckling turned into a swan."

"Only in fairy tales." The honesty in her eyes pained him. "My life isn't exactly a fairy tale, Max."

"I'm sorry it didn't turn out the way you'd expected."

"I'm not complaining."

"You never would."

He leaned over her shoulder and set the brush down near the sink. Her eyes met his in the mirror and held him spellbound. How could he imagine going back to his ranch in Arizona without her? This moment would be locked in his memory forever. Every time he looked in a mirror he would see her face instead of his own. Losing her again would be a torture he couldn't endure.

Max kept his gaze riveted on Liza Jane as he moved back and silently drew her hair aside. He lowered his head and kissed her neck.

When he returned his attention to her reflection, he asked, "Who do you see looking at you right now?"

Her lips curved in a bewildered grin. "You, of course."

He wrapped his fingers lightly around her upper arms and brought her to her feet, then turned her to face him. "Who did you see making love to you last night?"

"You," she answered cautiously, her faltering smile telling him differently.

"Was it really me?" He watched her closely. "Or were you wishing it was Johnny?"

Her eyelids squeezed shut as she gave an adamant shake of her head. "Absolutely not." She opened her eyes and gazed into his. "You are not John."

"I know... and I'm sorry."

She touched his clean-shaven chin. "Don't do this to yourself. You can't replace him and I don't want you to."

"What about last night? You wanted to pretend..."

"That you were John?" she asked, a light of understanding dawning in her eyes. "Oh, no! I never meant for you to think... When I came into your room, I thought I could prove to you that all there is between us is teenage memories of passionate sex and nothing more. But I started to lose my nerve, so I pretended we were in the hayloft in your barn."

He leaned forward and pressed a kiss against her lips, then rested his forehead against hers. "This is more than just memories."

"Is it?" Her lack of belief, her uncertainty knifed through him. Even if she didn't sense the bond between them, he did.

He gazed into her upturned face. "You and I were never good at playing games. We usually said what we meant."

"Which is why we fought all the time."

"I was about to say, when we try to pretend anything, we screw it up. I didn't realize you were pretending to be reliving our past. You didn't realize I was pretending to be Johnny because I thought that's what you wanted."

She dropped her chin to her chest, shaking her head.

"Don't be mad."

Her head shot up, her green eyes brimming with tears. "How can I be mad? You sacrificed your pride for me."

"That's not exactly how I'd put it," he said, uncomfortable with the heroic image of himself. Absent-mindedly toying with the lapels of her robe, he moved his hands up to her shoulders.

"You're not John," she repeated.

"We've covered that territory."

She reached up and grasped his hands with her own. "John was not you. He couldn't fill your shoes any more that you can fill his now. Do you remember how he was, Max?" She searched his face before continuing. "He was soft-spoken and very shy, especially with girls. He only pretended to be like you when you were around. But with me... he was sweet and considerate and—"

"I don't need to know the details of your relationship," Max said tersely, dragging his hands from her grasp.

"Please, Max. I need you to understand."

He forced himself to remain, wondering what kind of man would put himself through this kind of pain. *Obviously a man in love,* he heard a voice saying in the back of his head.

Liza Jane took a steadying breath. "John was deeply affected by his father's abusiveness toward his mother. In his effort to avoid the same behavior, he gravitated to the opposite extreme over the years. He was almost Victorian in his attitudes about marriage. In many ways, he was very old-fashioned."

"I assume that means even in the bedroom."

"Especially in bed." She sighed sadly. "Except that one disastrous evening at his mother's house, he didn't touch me again until after our wedding. And then it was only in bed. Only at night. Only under the covers."

"Sounds... boring."

She immediately straightened her spine defensively. "It was not boring."

"Okay, okay. Put the boxing gloves away. I was just making an assumption. A wrong one, apparently."

"I only told you about John so you'd realize that I didn't fantasize about him last night. You two were as different as—"

"Night and day?" he offered lightly.

She nodded, releasing his hands. "Precisely."

"Good."

"Good?"

"Yes, because it's broad daylight and I'm not about to wait until tonight... in bed... under the covers... to make love to you again." He untied her robe and slipped his hands beneath the material to grasp her waist.

"Here?" She glanced down at the tile floor. "In the bathroom?"

"Right here. Right now."

"I don't think we can."

"Let me be the judge of that." He peeled the white terry cloth from her shoulders, allowing it to fall to the slick surface of the counter behind her. "You are so beautiful," he whispered in a husky breath, dipping his head to her breast.

Elizabeth felt his mouth close around her nipple and gasped at the pleasure of his tongue flicking the sensitive tip.

Beautiful? Had he really said she was beautiful? She gazed at the top of his dark head, his eyes closed. Her fingers moved of their own accord, cupping the back of his skull, holding him to her. He moved to the other breast, suckling and tugging until she mewed like a kitten.

Tilting her head back, she looked up at the ceiling and reveled in the moment. Every muscle, every cell in her body quivered with anticipation. His mouth traveled lower as he knelt down.

Her fingers gripped the edge of the counter. With the ease and grace of a man who knew how to please a woman, he kissed her in the most intimate manner, touching her with his tongue in ways that made her feel exquisitely alive, soaring higher than birds could fly.

Somewhere out in the stratosphere, she floated for an instant on the wings of fulfillment, vaguely aware of Max rising to his feet. She opened her heavy lids with great effort, reaching out for him. Fumbling miserably with his belt buckle, she cursed her clumsy fingers.

"Slow down, hot stuff. Wouldn't want you to damage the goods." Chuckling to himself, he brought his mouth down on hers. As his hands cupped her bare bottom, his tongue distracted her from her mission.

"Hurry it up down there," he gently commanded.

"Slow down? Hurry up?" she repeated, tugging his briefs downward. "What do you want from me?"

"This," he answered impatiently. Kissing her, he shifted her bottom to the edge of the vanity, drew her legs around his hips and entered her fully.

CHAPTER 14

"I THINK WE OVERDID IT." Elizabeth said loudly over the plane engines.

Max laughed, glancing across at her with a lecherous grin. "There is no such thing as too much sex."

"I am not talking about *us*." She tipped her head toward the cargo hold. "I am talking about *that*."

Boxes of flood-relief supplies, stacked to the ceiling, filled every inch of space, along with *ten* water pumps. They only needed one. After Max learned of another supplier, he plunked down his credit card, despite the exorbitant markup. Surprised by his generosity, Elizabeth tried to talk him into buying only five. He argued he could buy two hundred and still not have enough to save family homes and businesses along the river.

Her headset slipped down again, prompting her to readjust them over her ears. She positioned the microphone in front of her mouth. "I was talking about the water pumps."

"You were?" His mirthful eyes glanced her way, then returned to the dark sky ahead. "Here I was thinking about you and me and one hell of a weekend we just spent together. If I didn't have a couple of new pumps to deliver, I'd have been happy to spend a year in that suite and never come out."

Me, too.

The realization surprised her, slipping past all the barriers she had tried to keep intact over the last several days. Unable to answer him, she turned her head and looked out the passenger window of the Beech-17. The weather was getting worse by the minute.

How could she make a lifetime commitment after only two days? Sure, the sex was great. Phenomenally great. But the Cinderella weekend was over. The glass slippers were off. She gazed down at her canvas tennis shoes, only to feel the tender ache at the apex of her thighs. The sweet soreness of their love-making had caught up to her. Never had she been so thoroughly exhausted in such a wonderful way.

"Why so quiet?" he asked over the drone of the engines.

"Just thinking."

"No regrets?"

She looked at him and smiled awkwardly. "None."

"Good. Me, neither."

"Now, why doesn't that surprise me?" she asked, drawing a smirk from him. "Try not to look too smug. Especially around Bernice."

"No point worrying about her finding out about us. She's already put two and two together and come up with four."

Elizabeth groaned, dropping her head back.

"And she gave her blessing."

"What?" She sat bolt upright. "You talked to Bernice about us?"

He nodded.

"What did you tell her?"

"This isn't exactly the place I'd planned to discuss the subject," he said, the noise from the plane reverberating around them.

"If I have to face Bernice the minute we land, I don't see how

147

you have any choice but to tell me now." Hollering over the engine roar wasn't the only reason her voice sounded shrill. "What did you say to her about us?"

A bolt of lightning zigzagged through the dark sky in front of the plane. She let out a startled yelp. His only reflex was a slight flinch.

Instead of competing with the deafening thunderclaps and engine noise, Max just glanced at her. The calm reassurance in his eyes spoke volumes, comforting her, easing her fears and tugging on her heart.

"That was too close," she murmured, her hand over her chest.

During the harrowing flight through the electrical storm, Elizabeth silently watched Max calmly handle the pressure with professional concentration. Even though he undoubtedly thrived on the adrenaline rush of such adventures, this was not the "Wildman" who drove like a bat out of hell after drinking a case of beer. This wasn't the brooding James Dean who didn't give a thought for anyone's safety, least of all his own. Somewhere along the way, he had found a way to harness the reckless teenager while keeping a little of wild streak hovering just beneath the surface. Enough to make him fascinating. Enough to make him passionate. Enough to make her love him. And that alone broke her heart, because she couldn't have him.

She had danced with the devil for a weekend, taken a selfish forty-eight hours for herself, but now reality was only an hour away. Once she went home to John's house, John's children and John's mother, the fairy tale would end.

AFTER SAFELY DELIVERING the bulk of flood-relief supplies in Saint Louis, the Beech-17 landed on the crude airstrip at the farmhouse. As Max shut down the engines of the hulking aircraft, he watched Liza Jane out of the corner of his eye. She had white-knuckled the worst of the flight and he was proud of her. The turbulence was enough to make a seasoned pro drop to his knees and kiss the ground. She had held on to her meager lunch, which was more than he could say about her breakfast that morning. He noticed that her stomach couldn't seem to handle food in any significant amount. It worried him. Every time he tried to discuss his concern, she cut him off. He did manage to learn that she was under the care of a local doctor, and that there was no physical problem, such as a stomach ulcer, that would upset her delicate system. Still, something wasn't right. There was more to her dwindling weight than a poor appetite.

A handful of women and children descended the back steps of the farmhouse, about a hundred yards north of the end of the airstrip. As the welcoming committee headed in their direction, Max could see Mrs. Mac walking arm-in-arm with Annie. Then he spotted a tall, thin figure hanging back, arms crossed and leaning against the porch post. Max hadn't expected Brodie to drive out from town to greet them, especially the way they'd left things. He didn't suppose the boy was too happy about his mother's decision to stay in Chicago, either.

Taking off his headphones, Max motioned toward the small army with a tilt of his head. "You go on ahead. I've got a few things to check out on the plane before we unload these water pumps."

"We're going to need some help."

"Brodie's here."

"He's just a boy. He can't muscle those crates around."

Max was tempted to remind her that her boy wasn't little anymore, but he thought better of it. "I'm sure Tug and Steve wouldn't mind helping out."

"I'll make some phone calls."

"Thanks."

When neither of them moved, he finally cleared his throat.

"You probably ought to know I told Mrs. Mac that I intend to get back together with you."

Elizabeth slumped against the seat. "How could you, Max? John has been gone only two years. I realize she gave her blessing to you, but did it ever occur to you that she might not be ready to see her son's widow with a new man in her life?"

"I'm not exactly some stranger who materialized out of nowhere. She thinks of me like a son. I think you're using your mother-in-law as an easy out. You're the only one having a problem about us."

"Can you blame me?"

"No—yes, dammit! I want to marry you. And if you could only see past this heap of guilt you've piled on yourself like so much horse sh—"

"I don't need to hear this," she snapped, unbuckling her safety belt and bolting from the passenger seat.

Throwing off his own seat belt, he followed her to the door of the plane. "You don't *need* to hear me? Or is it that you don't *want* to hear me?"

Refusing to answer him, she reached for the door handle, but he stepped between her and the door. "You and I are going to clear the air while we've still got some privacy."

"Leave me alone."

"No! You're going to hear me out."

"Looks like I don't have any choice."

"I spent the entire weekend making love to you—"

"It was sex, Max," she interjected. "We can't base an entire life-time together on just great sex."

Plowing his fingers through his hair, he muttered an oath. "It was *love*, Liza Ja— Oh, excuse me—*Elizabeth*."

"Don't make fun of my name."

"I'm *not!* I'm trying to remember to use it. Out of respect to you. I realize you are not Liza Jane anymore. I know you've changed. So have I. But that doesn't mean I'm giving up on us. I love you. I've always loved you. I can't just shut it off. Even *you* have got to know that!"

"I don't know any such thing," she argued with too much vehemence, too much denial. "When John married me, I *stopped* loving you."

He lifted one eyebrow skeptically. "Did you really?"

"I made a vow."

"Not in your heart."

"Yes, in my heart! I quit loving you and I fell in love with John. Why can't you accept that?" Her fists clenched at her sides. Tears spilled down her cheeks.

He took a step forward and gathered her into his arms. She tried to squirm out of his embrace. When she failed, she pummeled his chest with blows too weak to cause any damage, but strong enough to vent her anger at him. Finally, she collapsed against him, sobs wracking her body.

"I know you loved Johnny," he said soothingly, stroking her hair, then kissing the top of her head. "It tears me up inside that you loved him more than you ever loved me. But it's killing me to see you like this. You're wasting away, sweetheart. You need help getting over Johnny's death."

"And I suppose you're the one to help me. Is that what this whole weekend was about—helping the poor widow get over her grief?"

"You needed some time to rest, get away from all you have to deal with. Maybe I was stupid to assume a few days in Chicago would get you back on your feet."

"I was standing on my own two feet just fine until you came around."

"You've handled a lot, I'll give you that," he said gently. "You've raised some great kids, according to Mrs. Mac. You've helped her open the women's shelter. But what have you done for yourself?"

"I don't need to do anything for myself."

Gripping her slender arms, he leaned back to look down on

her. "You *do* need to take care of yourself. Something's awfully wrong if you can't hold down enough food to keep a parakeet alive. I want you to get some professional counseling. I'm going to see to it that you get the best in the country. I don't care where you have to go or how long it takes, I'm footing the bill."

"No!" She shoved herself away. "I'm not taking your money and I'm not going to any psychoanalyst who's going to show me ink blots and tell me I'm depressed." She stepped around him and stood defiantly next to the door. "Now let me out of here so I can get back to the boarding house with that pump."

Max released a pent-up sigh of frustration. "You're one damn stubborn woman, Liza Jane."

"Elizabeth," she corrected through gritted teeth.

~

A HALF HOUR LATER, Elizabeth paced the length of the old wooden porch, checking her watch for the third time. Bernice sat on the front stoop snapping green beans with a small partner, a little girl of four who belonged to a new boarder. The child had tight cornrow braids that bobbed as she moved her dark head.

"They ought to be here by now," Elizabeth muttered, tired and exasperated that the two men had yet to show up to haul the pump.

"Give them time. There're more roads flooded since you left on Saturday," her mother-in-law patiently explained. "I don't know why you're so fired up to get that pump down to the boarding house. Another hour or two won't hurt either way."

"You sound like Max."

"Maybe he's right"

"And maybe I can't go upstairs and just fall asleep like he did."

"He's exhausted from all that flying."

More than just flying, Elizabeth thought, ready to collapse from her own marathon weekend.

Bernice finished the vegetables and handed the stainless-steel bowl to the child, instructing her to take it to her mother working in the kitchen. When the little girl eagerly departed, Bernice pushed herself to her feet, smoothed the floral kitchen smock with her hands, then plunged them into the deep front pockets.

Turning to Elizabeth, she walked up the steps. "I understand Max offered to help you."

"He's helped enough already, flying all the way to Chicago for that water pump."

"I wasn't talking about the pump." She came over to Elizabeth, stopped and leaned back against the handrail of the porch. "What do you think of his suggestion?"

"About therapy?" When her mother-in-law nodded, Elizabeth shook her head. "The only thing wrong with me right now is a bad case of Boomerang Boyfriend."

Bernice laughed. "I'm glad to see you still have your sense of humor."

"Not with him I don't."

"Come here," she beckoned, extending her open palm. Elizabeth stepped forward and took her mother-in-law's hand. "For two years I've been watching you waste away like prairie grass drying up in the hot sun. Then along comes Maxwell—"

"The burning match if ever there was one," Elizabeth grumbled. Bernice grinned, patting the top of her hand.

"I was thinking of him as a refreshing summer rain."

"Max? Hardly!" Maybe a summer storm, complete with deafening thunder and white-hot lightning bolts. Instead of the two turbulent flights leaping to the forefront of her mind, she was thinking of the electrically charged passion they had shared in the hotel suite.

A beat-up blue pickup truck ambled up the rural road, drawing their attention.

"Good, they're here." Elizabeth lifted her free hand and waved.

The two men in the front seat returned the greeting as they pulled into the driveway. She motioned them around to the back of the house and began to follow.

Bernice lightly squeezed Elizabeth's hand. "One more thing before you take off..."

"Yes?"

"Most women thank their lucky stars to have one good man to call their own, never mind two in a lifetime. You think on that."

~

"WHAT DO YOU MEAN, SHE'S GONE?" Max was about to take a bite of a ham sandwich prepared for him by one of his new house-guests when he got the news from Brodie. The boy sat across the kitchen table, silently devouring his second sandwich with the sort of hollow-leg enthusiasm that only a growing teenager could do. He reminded Max of himself a few years back. Quite a few.

With a muffled response around a mouthful of food, Brodie answered indifferently. "She followed Tug and Steve back to town after they loaded the pump, about an hour ago."

"Followed? In what—my truck?"

"Her own car," he said smugly. "I replaced the battery while you two were... gone."

Max bit through the bread and meat, ripping off a chunk and chewing it hard. All he'd wanted was to unwind from the tense flight before driving into town with the new water pump. But she couldn't wait to inspect the flood damage to the shelter. She would rather make a useless attempt to save the already flooded building than grant him a few hours' rest.

Max felt Brodie's eyes on him before he actually looked up from his plate to see the boy staring. "You got something to say to me, say it."

With eyes narrowed, Brodie put down the sandwich and

dropped his arms on the table, his anger simmering just beneath the surface.

"If I was a few years older," he muttered, his voice too low to be heard by anyone but Max, "I'd make sure you never came around my mom ever again. I already got in two fights yesterday because of what kids are saying about you and her. She does not need you flying her off on fancy weekends at fancy hotels—not with the way people talk. As far as I'm concerned, you can go to hell."

CHAPTER 15

*B*RODIE LEVERED HIMSELF TO HIS FEET, shoved the chair back and headed into the living room. Max heard the television come on and channels being flipped until it settled on a music video.

The boy made no bones about it—he hated Max with a passion. Max stared at the doorway leading into the living room, then shook his head in disappointment.

Somehow, someway, he and Brodie would have to come to an understanding or come to blows. He didn't know which it would be, but he sure hoped he wasn't going to go up against Liza Jane's son in a fist fight. He'd do anything to avoid that sort of confrontation. In the meantime, he had more important things on his mind—the kid's mother. The two of them hadn't exactly ended their fly-away weekend together on a cordial note, and he aimed to remedy the situation right away.

He gulped down the last of his milk, set the glass on the table and scooped up the other half of his sandwich. Heading across the kitchen toward the back door, he paused and glanced back at his dirty dishes. He wasn't living in his bachelor digs anymore, leaving his own mess lying around until he got around to cleaning it up. Just as he was about to reach for the tumbler and plate, Bernice entered the room from the cellar door, her arms loaded with a large wicker basket full of wet laundry.

"Never mind those dishes," she said, huffing and puffing. Beads of sweat glistened across her forehead. "I could use some of your help hanging these sheets."

"Did the dryer quit?"

"The dryer's been doing double duty since yesterday morning, and it's as hot as Hades down there. So I figured these sheets could hang outside."

"What if it rains? There's dark clouds coming this way."

"In this heat, I'll be taking down the first one as soon as I finish putting up the last. Besides, I happen to prefer the fresh-air smell on my sheets." She handed over the basket with a grunt. "Lord, these legs aren't what they used to be. There was a time when this ol' girl could climb up and down stairs a hundred times without a single joint cracking. Now I sound like a gosh-darn popcorn kettle."

Max smiled at Bernice, enjoying her sense of humor and the twinkle in her ageless eyes. He had missed her over the years nearly as much as his own mom.

"Outside with you now." She shooed him with a flap of her hands.

As they approached the rusted metal T-posts between the barn and house, Max noticed the white plastic clothesline. "Who put up the new line?"

"Brodie. He's been helping out quite a lot over the weekend."

"So I heard." Max stopped near the hanging clothespin bag and held the basket waist high for her to reach the sheets without bending over. "He says he put a new battery in the car, too."

"Wasn't that sweet of him?" She rummaged for the end of a sheet.

"Yeah. . . Real sweet. I also heard Li—Elizabeth took her car back to town." *Without me.*

Bernice reached into the bag and pulled out a couple of wooden clothespins. "She was eager to get that pump up and running, though goodness knows it won't do much good at this point."

"Doesn't she seem a little too..."

"Obsessed?"

"I suppose that about says it."

Bernice kept her eyes on the task of lifting and pegging the wet laundry securely into place as Max shifted sideways to keep up with her progress.

Continuing her pace, she thoughtfully explained, "Elizabeth is at a real important turning point in her life. After John's death, she devoted herself to restoring that old building with the same sort of commitment she gave her marriage. Even though I'm glad I asked her to help me fix up the place, I can see now that she might be a tad too attached to it, as if it's somehow her last direct connection to my son."

"She's holding on to that building as a way of holding on to Johnny?"

Bernice nodded. She didn't look at him, just kept hanging sheets. "I'm not saying that this horrible flood is a blessing to those folks who lost everything. But as for Elizabeth... Well, we both need to let go of the past. Start over. Look ahead."

"You're a pretty smart lady."

"I just listen to what my heart tells me." She glanced up at him and winked. "Women's intuition."

"What's your women's intuition tell you about Elizabeth closing that door to the past? Especially with me hanging around as a constant reminder?"

Max waited for a response as the last clothespin was silently clipped into place. Bernice pivoted toward him and lightly rested her hands next to his on the rim of the basket.

"Don't give up on her, Maxwell," she gently pleaded. "I told you before and I'll say it again—you are like a son to me, and I want to see you two kids work this out."

Max nodded. "Thank you, ma'am."

She dropped her hands into the pockets of her apron. "You use to call me *Mom*."

"I also used to swipe chocolate-chip cookies off the kitchen counter that were meant for the church bake sale."

"I know."

"You did?" He eyed her suspiciously as she turned back toward the house. The empty wicker basket hung from one hand, bumping against his left leg. "Why didn't you stop me?"

"Because you called me *Mom*." She smiled and he saw a telltale glisten in her eyes. "Underneath all that swaggering, tough-guy image that had the girls in a dither, you were a good boy, I knew."

"Not exactly the popular opinion at the time."

"Maybe not," she answered, walking up the back steps and entering the kitchen. "But you proved them all wrong, didn't you?"

"I wouldn't know. I haven't been on the ground long enough to catch up on the town gossip."

"As soon as you have more than a half hour between all these flood-relief flights, you just might find yourself hauled into the town hall for a ceremony of commendation in your honor."

At first, he thought she was joking, but then he saw something impish, something akin to pride on her face. "Tell the mayor to forget about me and hand out plaques to everybody who worked the pumps and filled the sandbags. They're the heroes, not me."

"That sounds like a pretty good start for your acceptance speech." With a bright expression, she reached for the basket. "Now, if you'll excuse me, I've got oodles of work waiting for me. I hope I didn't keep you from anything important."

His mind was still contemplating the ridiculous notion of a ceremony in his honor when the course of the conversation jumped tracks. It took him a moment to recover his thoughts.

"I wasn't heading anywhere important. Just thought I'd check on that new water pump."

"I suppose Elizabeth will still be there."

"S'pose so."

"Letting go is never easy."

"Never is." He went to the door and grabbed his hat off the rack.

"I hope I gave you something to chew on until you get there."

"You certainly did, ma'am." He saw her disappointed expression and offered her an apologetic grin. "Bye... Mom."

He dropped his hat on his head and walked out the back door, feeling pretty good about the smile he'd left on her face.

MAX DROVE PAST FLOODED farmland that had been dry the week before. His truck followed roads that had been untouched a few days earlier but were now under two to four inches of water that had seeped between rows of wet sandbags. Muddy volunteers, too many to count, worked in straggling groups. While heavy rains still pounded the northern states, the river would continue to rise. Rumors were rampant about new levees failing as quickly as old ones.

His gaze briefly scanned the afternoon sky, noting the slow-moving thunderheads coming down from the north. Nothing seemed to be able to stop the changing course of the river.

Not even Liza Jane.

She was as determined to fight the force of nature as all the other flood-relief workers filling sandbags night and day. Could he blame her for trying desperately to save the old boarding house, to save this one thing, this one connection to Johnny?

Even though the McKenzie building had initially been a welcome diversion from grief, it had come to mean more to her. She needed to be willing to let go of the brick house in order to let go of the past. Hadn't she said the same about him? He was a part of her past, a part she no longer wanted. With painful acceptance, he began to understand what she had meant about their intimate weekend. It had been about sex, pure and simple. She'd proven her point. Together, their physical attraction was a powder keg of sexual fireworks. She saw bursting rockets, not love. Just lust, she'd admitted to him. Nothing more.

"Dammit!" He smacked the palm of his hand against the steering wheel. It was time to get it over with. It was time to say goodbye.

~

AFTER A BRIEF STOP TO DROP off her daughter at a friend's house, Elizabeth discovered the river was almost at the foundation of the boarding house. Despite the work of the two remaining pumps, the vast basement was nearly full of water seeping through the saturated ground, finding its way between every crack and crevice. She lost the battle. Even though she learned the truth on Saturday night from Brodie, she didn't believe it until she saw it for herself.

Defeated and alone, she stood on the step at the top of the cellar stairs as the first silent tear fell. The crest of the flood was expected to reach far beyond the level it had in 1993. Within twenty-four hours, this very step would probably be under the murky water, polluted by the stench of chemicals and waste. The flood carried everything in its path, dredging up long-buried caskets, oil drums and septic tanks. There was nothing sterile about the devastation. She stared down at the black, muddy water, realizing the additional help of the new pump would not stop the tide of tragedy.

Elizabeth turned around and left the basement, closing the door behind her—as if it mattered anymore. The thin wooden door wouldn't hold back the water when the level rose above the foundation. She swiped at her cheek with her palm, scrubbing the tears from her face.

Going from room to room, from first floor to second, she felt as if she were saying goodbye to an old friend, not knowing if the historic building could withstand the damage that was yet to come. Downstairs had been emptied of all furnishings, many of them moved into upstairs bedrooms.

She entered one of those rooms, wound her way past chairs and occasional tables, a wingback library chair and a double bed stripped of its linen. The late-afternoon sun rode low between the horizon and a ceiling of rain clouds that had followed her into town. Pale light streamed through a tall, narrow window. Without its ruffled muslin curtains, the opening looked barren, the glass panes dulled by a thin film of dust and grime.

Through the window, she gazed out upon the endless swath of muddy brown water. Memories swept by as fast as the flooded river. Memories of a lonely childhood, of wanting nothing more than to feel loved and wanted. Like her own son, she had been an unexpected baby. But Elizabeth had never enjoyed the same unconditioned love that she showered on Brodie. Instead, she'd learned quite young that she was only a shameful reminder of a foolish mistake. There had been little joy in her home, which was why she'd sought the excitement and thrills of being with Wildman.

She remembered the way he skidded up to her house as she ran out the front door, her mom yelling at her to be home by midnight. Max would be grinning that devilishly handsome grin when she hopped into the seat next to him. Then he peeled out, scattering gravel in their wake. Elizabeth could almost feel her heart racing in her chest the way it did back then, recalling the way he hauled her into his lap while tearing down a back road at breakneck speed. She'd scream. He'd laugh, then kiss her, closing his eyes for a bone-chilling moment. They were crazy. They were foolish. They were two teenagers who didn't believe death could ever catch up to them.

But it had caught up to John.

"Oh, John..." She sighed, sadness filling her chest and tightening her throat. Her eyes stung with the sudden return of overwhelming grief. The past two years vanished in that moment, bringing back the heartache of losing her husband. Though these episodes of loneliness occurred less frequently with each passing month, when they came upon her unexpectedly, they were no less gut-wrenching than the first few weeks following the plane crash.

She reached up and braced her hand against the window frame as she tried to gather her strength about her like a tattered robe.

"How could you leave me?" she asked aloud. "We had our whole life ahead of us, you and me. We were so happy. . . finally. After all those years that you put up with me—with my selfish moods, with my self-pity, with my self-hatred."

Her fingers gripped the frame, squeezing it tighter as she squeezed her eyes shut, trying to stop the tears. She dropped her chin to her chest and a silent sob shook her body. But she held on, willing herself to maintain control as she had done so many times before.

"Why, John? Why did you go and leave me behind? I depended on you, on your advice. What am I to do now? Look at the mess I've created! And with Max, of all people. I broke my promise."

The vacant room mocked her with silence. How she longed for John to materialize out of thin air and wrap his arms around her, telling her that everything would be fine. That had been her dream, her fantasy for the past two years. Sometimes she actually believed he was in the room with her. Sometimes her skin warmed as if he had really hugged her and comforted her.

"I still love you, John. But heaven help me, I love Max, too." She looked out over the miles-wide ribbon of water.

Confusion and turmoil clouded her mind. She saw herself swept away in the events of the past week like a drowning victim battling the swift water. Far away on the distant shore, she thought she could see a tiny speck, a lone figure waving frantically at her.

With the palm of her hand, Elizabeth cleaned the center pane of glass in an ever-widening circle, until the grime framed a clear view. The shadowy figure could have been anyone, yet she sensed a disturbing familiarity. Her heart began to pound with anticipation and fear.

"John?" she whispered hoarsely, afraid to believe the illusion, yet wanting to with all her heart. "Johnny?"

Time and space lost all perspective as her eyes focused on the masculine form. He seemed to be throwing a rescue rope toward her. The vague image grew more distinct with each deafening beat of her heart.

"I know it sounds crazy that I could love both of you all these years. But I know I made you happy. You said so."

The visionary figure standing on the riverbank threw the rescue rope one more time, then waited as the lifeline drifted toward her.

Elizabeth reached out, only to have her hands flatten on the glass barrier of the window. Startled by the jarring reality, she gasped, shutting her eyes to the mirage, shutting out the pain.

A strange sensation came over her, then the familiar warmth she had longed for spread down her body. A sense of peace eased the fear in her bones.

Her eyes flew open. For the breadth of a long moment, she saw the serene face of her husband. Somehow, she knew he wanted her to grab hold of the rope. She imagined the scratchy wet hemp against her fingers and palms. His smile conveyed goodbye. He'd given his blessing. Her heart ached with both relief and sadness.

"Don't go!" she murmured, but his features wavered like a watery illusion.

Only then did Elizabeth realize that a steady drizzle had begun to fall from the dark canopy of clouds. What little was left of the mystical sunset was swallowed up by the gray sky.

She touched the glass where, in her mind's eye, she could still see John. There, in the window, was another face.

Max?

It was Max standing on the shore. It was Max holding the other end of the rope. It was Max pulling her toward the safety of the riverbank. For the first time, Elizabeth saw him not as the destructive force of floodwaters, she had imagined, but as a man fighting to save her. A man she could finally allow herself to love.

≈

MAX STOOD IN THE DOORWAY of the upstairs bedroom, holding his hat in his hands. Liza Jane was lost in her own world and unaware of his presence. Her dark blond hair was pulled back at the nape of her neck and fell in a soft ponytail down her back. She wore a sleeveless denim blouse tucked into a pair of jeans that could have fit tighter around her slim little bottom. He allowed himself to memorize her reflection in the windowpane. Her large green eyes. Her slightly turned-up nose. Her full lips. This picture of her would have to last him a lifetime. When thoughts of losing her tightened his chest, he forced himself to step into the room.

"Elizabeth?"

With a startled squeak of surprise, she spun around to see him standing in the doorway. After a quick glance at the window, she turned back toward him, confusion in her eyes. "How long have you been standing there?"

He couldn't admit that he'd been staring at her for what seemed like an eternity. Yet even now, it hadn't been long enough. "I just got here."

"Oh..." She seemed at a loss for words. "I wasn't expecting you."

"I would've called..."

"But the phones are out," she finished for him, shoving her hands in the front pockets of her jeans.

"I saw Tug outside. He says the new pump is up and working. Looks like you've got everything under control."

She gave him a strange look he couldn't quite figure out. "Yeah... It looks that way."

"That's good." The conversation between them was noticeably awkward. "Well, I just came by to say goodbye. I'll be flying out in the morning."

"Already?" Was it disappointment he saw in her eyes? "When will you be back?"

"I won't," he answered with a shortness he hadn't intended. He fingered the brim of his hat. "I'm going to be puddle-jumpin' from here on out, going where I'm needed most. In a few more weeks I ought to be able to head back home to Arizona."

Neither one of them said a word as they stared at each other in the silent room.

"Liza Jane... Elizabeth?"

"Yes?"

"I..."

Don't say it, Wilder. Don't tell her you love her. Keep it inside. Don't let her see the pain. Not again.

She prompted, "Yes? What do you want to tell me?"

He had to get out of here fast, before he broke down and made a total ass of himself. With little more than a wave of his hat, he murmured, "Take care of yourself, Elizabeth."

Max turned toward the open doorway.

CHAPTER 16

"*W*AIT!" MAX COULD HEAR Elizabeth bumping into furniture, but he wouldn't stop even though it was killing him to walk away. She caught up with him in the hall, darting in front of him and blocking his path. He hoped to hell she couldn't see the damn tears in his eyes.

"I *need* you, Max."

He remembered the afternoon she'd stood on his porch and said those same words. Was it only a few days ago? He felt as if he'd lived his whole life in the span of this last week. This time when she said she needed him, he didn't misunderstand her meaning. She was still desperately trying to save this building—her husband's legacy.

"I did what you asked. The water pump's been delivered. You don't need me anymore."

Shaking her head, she stepped forward, narrowing the space between them. She tipped up her chin, her green eyes dark and intent.

"It's too late to save the boarding house, Max."

"You're not giving up, are you? Not after all you've done."

"I'm letting go."

Max felt his knees nearly buckle, but he was scared to death to hope. "But you were so determined to save your family's heritage."

"It's not my heritage, not really. After the flood recedes, I'll still try to do what I can to help rebuild it. But I'll do it for Bernice and for my children—not for John. Not for me."

"I could cover costs."

"You don't need to do that."

"I won't miss it," he responded flippantly, hoping to end the refusal. After all, it was the least he could do after walking back into her life and throwing her world into a tailspin. "I could use the tax break."

Elizabeth shook her head. Once more she'd made a mess of things. She couldn't let Max leave, not when she finally realized he would be walking out of her life forever.

"I don't need your money." She stepped closer and placed her palms on his chest. "I need *you*." Her fingers slid upward, then around his neck. "Now."

"Now?" His Adam's apple bobbed in his throat. Wildman was downright flustered, which pleased Elizabeth no end. One way or the other she was going to convince him that he was the man she wanted. She knew it was a crazy risk to seduce him in the hallway of the empty boarding house, especially while the volunteers were manning the pumps. Yet it was her last chance to prove that she was truly in love with him. She pressed her body against his. "Please, Max..."

"Don't start that begging routine on me again."

Elizabeth lifted her eyebrows in feigned innocence, aware of his physical response to their ageless game. "Am I bothering you?"

"Hell, yes, you're bothering me. I didn't come here for one last roll in the sack. I wouldn't do that to you."

"You wouldn't?"

"No, dammit! I don't want to leave you thinking that sex was the only reason I wanted you."

"I don't."

"Good."

"Is your conscience clear now?"

He eyed her suspiciously. "About as clear as it's gonna get." Slowly, he removed her hands from around his neck. Elizabeth felt a moment of panic but refused to be put off.

"Make love to me," she purred, unfastening the snap at the top of his jeans. "Right here." The zipper slid down. "Right now."

Her fingers slipped between the elastic waistband and his hard, flat stomach. Her own boldness surprised her. Yet she couldn't deny the mad rush of adrenaline that shot through her body. In another brazen move, she knelt in front of Max.

"Holy—" His words died in a gasp. His hat fell to the floor beside him. His fingers clasped the back of her head. "What are you doing to me?"

Elizabeth smiled to herself and continued her blatant seduction. A few minutes later he coaxed her to her feet, then lowered his mouth to hers. After a long, deep kiss, he pulled her to him and held her tightly in his arms. His heart pounded against her chest.

He whispered into her hair. "We shouldn't be doing this."

"I know." She slipped her hands between their bodies and unfastened her own jeans, then pushed them down over her hips. His swollen flesh pressed wantonly against her smooth belly.

"This is crazy," he murmured, his breathing escalating.

"Extremely."

He took her hands and stepped back, shaking his head as if to clear away the confusion. "I've got to leave."

Elizabeth searched his face, remembering a similar moment in the hallway of his family farmhouse. "Don't stop. Not again."

The seconds ticked by as he stared into her eyes.

Without a word, he lifted Liza Jane into his arms and carried her into the cluttered bedroom. He closed the door with a hitch of his heel, then maneuvered an obstacle course toward the bed. When he placed her on the bare mattress, he reverently removed her clothes. As she lay naked, his fingertips caressed the soft skin of her shoulder, then lightly trailed between her small breasts, over her flat stomach.

"You are so beautiful. . . I. . ." She brought his hand to her lips, kissing the back of it.

"Come here," she murmured, her own eyes bright with tears. She reached up and cupped her hands around his neck, drawing his mouth down to hers. He moaned with pleasure as her wet tongue performed some incredible thrusts and withdrawals. His groin tightened with its own response. He started to pull away to remove the last of his own clothes, but she shook her head.

"Take me now, Max. Right now."

He knew it was risky, to say the least. Here they were, the two of them, hot as two teenagers parked on a deserted road at midnight. Only it was broad daylight. They were in a building in the middle of town. And the door was unlocked. It was crazy. But it made him even more aroused than he thought possible. Liza Jane wanted him. She couldn't wait for a nice, discreet rendezvous in a dark hotel room. She wanted him now.

A lazy smile slowly tilted up the corners of his mouth. "The least I can do is oblige a lady."

Her quiet giggle swept him back to the past. Damn, but it was the sweetest sound he could imagine.

A powerful need rose inside him. He pressed her down into the mattress as he shifted his weight, entering her with a force that shook him to his core. Her fingers dug into his buttocks, pulling him deeper.

Knowing they could be discovered at any second during their frenzied lovemaking, Max relished the senseless abandon of the woman in his arms. His heart swelled as he watched her throw her head back, her eyes squeezed shut in the throes of her physical pleasure. Her body quivered beneath him. Her muscles tightened around him. Only then did he allow his own explosive release.

Entwined in each other's embrace, they held on tightly, breathing in deep gulps of air.

"I love you, Max," she whispered, her voice raw with emotion.

He pulled back in surprise and gazed down at her. "What did you say?"

She smiled sheepishly. "I said I love you. I suppose I never stopped loving you. Not completely, anyway. But it wasn't until this afternoon that I finally realized I could love both you and John."

Max didn't care if the entire town walked into the room at that moment. He couldn't move, couldn't budge an inch as he listened to Liza Jane tell him about her experience at the window earlier.

"When you walked out of the room," she said in conclusion, "I couldn't bear the thought of losing you."

He brushed her bangs from her forehead and pressed his lips to her forehead. "You damn near broke my heart a second time, young lady."

"I'm not so young anymore."

"Bullsh—" He grinned apologetically. "You are as young as you make me feel. Right now I feel like a nineteen-year-old playing with the farmer's daughter out behind the barn. Do you realize we could get caught up here doing this?"

"Is Wildman worried?"

"Hell yes. You've got a reputation to uphold in this town."

Liza Jane gave him a playful shove, then rolled him onto his back and straddled his hips. "Then it looks like you'll have to make an honest woman of me."

"That's what I've been trying to do all along." When he saw a flicker of concern in her green eyes, he touched her cheek with the tips of his fingers. "What are you thinking about?"

"Brodie and Annie. They are my number-one priority, Max. You know that."

"We'll talk to them together. How about tomorrow night?"

"Come for dinner. We'll tell them afterward."

"Sounds good," he offered, then drew her down to him and kissed her again.

As her soft, wet, feminine flesh gently undulated over his manhood, he felt the tightness return. Her nude body moved in a slow seduction. He closed his eyes, allowing the sensation to wash over him like a warm tide. When he opened his eyes, he found her watching him intently, her eyelids heavy. Her chest heaved with each deep inhalation, her pert little breasts thrusting outward in brazen sexuality.

Welcome back, Liza Jane.

∿

THE FOLLOWING EVENING, Elizabeth heard the doorbell ring as she helped Bernice prepare dinner. Leaving the kitchen, she approached her front door with butterflies stirring in her stomach, taking her mind off any notion of eating even a bite. In the next instant, she stood with the door wide and her heart in her throat.

Max wore his black cowboy hat, a snug-fitting Western shirt in deep burgundy and black and a pair of brand-new blue jeans that had a nice neat crease clear down to the top of his cleaned-up cowboy boots. A little spit and polish did wonders for his rugged handsomeness. Only when he held out the small bouquet did she notice the wildflowers he was carrying—a mix of yellows, blues and pinks.

"They're beautiful!" Graciously taking the flowers, she stepped back to let him in. He removed his hat and held it by the brim as she gazed down at this simple yet touching gesture of his affection. "Where did you find them?"

"Russian's Field."

Her head snapped up. He grinned. He had not forgotten the place where they had spent many warm afternoons creating private and intimate memories.

"You went there?"

He glanced around the living room, then turned back and pressed a firm, possessive kiss on her lips. It happened so quickly she didn't have a chance to react, yet it left behind a flash fire of heat spiraling down her body, settling in the deep recesses of her belly. He withdrew a respectable distance as if he had been completely innocent of igniting such a bonfire. "I drove over there this afternoon."

She felt her heart swell. Burying her nose in the bouquet to mask her emotions, she inhaled the intoxicating fragrance and wished she were nuzzling his neck, inhaling his own familiar scent. How she wanted to rush through this special dinner so she could be alone with Max again. Now that she had finally sorted out her confused emotions, she couldn't seem to see enough of him. She would never get enough of him.

"I better put these in some water."

As he followed her through the living room, he left his hat lying on a side table. In the dining room, she glanced over her shoulder to see him take a quick survey of the fine heirloom china, polished silverware and white linen napkins on the table.

He gave a low whistle of awe. "You changed your mind about a casual dinner with your family."

Resting her hand on the swinging kitchen door, she gave him a nervous smile. "I changed my mind about a lot of things lately."

Entering the kitchen, Elizabeth noticed that Brodie was missing, and her uplifted spirits plummeted. He'd been there a minute ago. At the far counter by the refrigerator, her daughter paused in the middle of pouring milk into several tall glasses, then went back to her task, throwing an occasional covert glance in Max's direction.

Bernice removed her apron. "Well, now, aren't you a sight for these old tired eyes!" Beaming delightedly, she stood back with her hands on her hips and took in every inch of him. "You clean up real good, boy."

Max shifted his grin into high gear. "Thank you, Mrs. Mac —uh, Mom."

Elizabeth's gaze leaped from one to the other. Whatever was behind their brief, conspiratorial smiles would remain their own private secret, yet she couldn't help feeling her curiosity peak.

Bernice announced, "Let's get the show on the road."

"Where did Brodie run off to?" Elizabeth turned to her daughter. "Annie, why don't you go look in the garage?"

"Yes, ma'am," her nine-year-old answered reluctantly. Clearly smitten by the handsome Max Wilder, she backed out of the room, adoration in her eyes.

Like mother, like daughter. Elizabeth watched her, hoping her own attraction to the man was not so blatant. She was not used to the idea of him being in her life again. She felt like she was walking around in a glorious daze, forgetting where she put things, smiling at everyone she met.

When her dreamy-eyed daughter finally made it out the door, Elizabeth turned to Max. "Looks like you won her over."

"I have a tendency to do that to females." His cocky grin saved him from an admonishing swat on the arm, though Elizabeth was sorely tempted. Lord, he was a devil in tight jeans.

Max offered to help bring the food to the table, but Bernice shooed him out the door to the dining room. "Sit down. You're our guest," she ordered, commandeering Brodie and Annie for the task when they returned.

Fried chicken was not as elegant as a turkey with all the trimmings for a special occasion that called for a festive dinner, but a fancy meal would have been wasted on her. She was too nervous to eat. Max, on the other hand, was crazy about Bernice's home cooking. Apparently, her golden-brown chicken was his favorite food back in the days he spent at John's house.

As everyone finished eating, Elizabeth felt Max's hand slipped into hers under the table, unseen by anyone else. She was afraid to look at him, afraid her family would see right through her calm facade. Inside, she was happy, scared, excited, worried, and jittery. The gentle squeeze of his fingers gave her the reassurance she needed. She missed having a partner who could read her thoughts, share her feelings. John had been so good at that.

A twinge of guilt threatened to bring back the doubt and apprehension until she thought of her vision of him through the upstairs window of the boarding house. Real or imagined, he had released her to live her life without him. She believed he would be happy for her. And for Max.

"May I be excused?" Brodie started to rise from his chair to leave. She had been grateful for his polite, yet cool acceptance of their guest. Now it was time to face the music.

"Not yet." She touched her son's arm. "We'd like to have a family meeting."

Her son's eyes narrowed, then he jerked his head toward Max, sitting on the other side of her at the head of the table. "A family meeting doesn't include *him.*"

CHAPTER 17

WHILE ELIZABETH BRACED for the worst, she felt another little squeeze of her hand under the table. She took a deep breath. "As a matter of fact, Max *is* included."

"I've asked your mother to marry me," he stated calmly.

Brodie glared at Elizabeth. "I bet you said yes, didn't you?"

She looked at Max and her entire body flushed with the heat of desire, of need, of a love that she could no longer deny. She returned her gaze to her son and nodded. "Yes, I've accepted his proposal. I know it seems sudden, but I hope we have your blessing."—She glanced at Bernice and Annie—"All of you."

Bernice burst into tears. "You couldn't make me any happier than to see you two together."

"Annie?" Elizabeth eyed her daughter, hope in her heart. "What about you?"

Annie's smile of delight faltered as she gave her big brother a worried glance. "Will we have to move away from our friends?"

Silently berating herself for not having talked about that important issue, Elizabeth stammered, "We—we haven't begun to make those kinds of plans." She darted a look toward Max, seeking his help.

"I'm sure we can work something out," he said promptly. "You might enjoy Arizona. The ranch is pretty big. There are plenty of horses to ride. You could bring a friend along on summer vacations."

"You have horses?" The wide-eyed awe returned to Annie's face. "Would I have my very own pony?"

Brodie sneered. "Yeah, Squirt. Mister Millionaire will buy you anything you want. He's loaded. He'll spoil you rotten if you call him *Daddy*."

"Brodie!" Elizabeth exclaimed.

"I'm not your father and I don't expect to be called Dad," Max stated firmly.

"Good." The teen shoved himself up from his seat. "Don't expect me to bless this stupid marriage, either."

As he stalked out of the dining room, Elizabeth leaped to her feet, but Max reached out and gently grasped her wrist.

"I need to talk to him."

"Let me." He rose from his chair. "I've seen this coming. He and I have to reach some kind of truce before we can live under the same roof together."

He glanced around the table at the three female faces, all of them looking as though their family dog had just died. This wasn't a pleasant experience for him, either. If he couldn't make peace with Brodie, Liza Jane would never go through with the wedding.

"What are you going to say to him?" Liza Jane gazed at him, worry and uncertainty written in her eyes.

Max could see she was struggling with her need to run to her son, to ease his pain, to protect him. But he would only make her feel more guilt when she had every right to re-marry, to grab a chance at happiness.

"I don't know what we'll talk about," Max said honestly. "All I know is that it's high time we straightened out a few things between us." He touched her cheek to reassure her. "Don't worry.

We'll work all this out. I promise."

When he grinned with more confidence than he felt, she returned a weak smile of optimism.

A few minutes later, Max found the teenager brooding in the backyard, sitting on top of a weathered redwood picnic table, his feet on the bench. Realizing he'd been spotted, the boy hopped down and started toward the garage.

"We've got some talking to do," Max stated.

"Maybe you do but I don't."

"You're getting good at running off, aren't you?" challenged Max. "Is that how you handle everything these days—by running?"

Brodie turned and glared. "I don't run from anybody."

"You run from me."

"Well, maybe I'm just like my old man." He advanced, closing the distance between them.

"Johnny never ran away from his problems."

"I'm not talking about him." Brodie pointed an accusing finger at Max. "I'm talking about the son-of-a-bitch who ran off when Liza Jane Brown got pregnant!"

Masking his shock at the boy's angry accusation, Max recalled how easily he himself had jumped to the same conclusion. But he believed Liza Jane when she denied his paternity. Apparently, the boy hadn't bothered to check with his mom about the facts.

"I'm not your father."

"Liar!" yelled Brodie with a swing of his fist.

Caught by surprise, Max took a solid blow to his chin, his head whipping to the side. Restraining his reflex to defend himself, he moved his jaw back and forth with his hand. Near as he could tell, nothing was broken. His gaze settled on the teenager's fists raised for a fight.

Realizing the volcano was about to blow, Max chose his

words carefully. "When I first saw you, I was certain you were mine—and I was madder than hell that your mom never told me I had a son. But she set me straight."

"And you believed her?"

"Hell, yes! Your mama and I may have had our differences in the past, but I've never known her to lie about something as important as this. She swore to me that Johnny was your dad."

"Are you saying that Mom..." Brodie faltered as his anger escalated. "That *both* you and my dad..."

"It's not the way it sounds."

"Not *my* mom! She wasn't like that!"

When Brodie lunged forward again, Max dodged to the right. The fifteen-year-old fell face down in the damp, muddy grass.

Behind him, Max heard Liza Jane cry out, "Brodie!"

He turned to see her running across the yard, rushing to the boy sprawled on the ground. At the back stoop, Bernice stood behind Annie, her comforting arms wrapped around her granddaughter, holding her back as they watched from a distance.

Liza Jane helped her son to his feet, touching his stomach, his arms, his chin. "Are you all right?"

"Yeah," he muttered, awkwardly withdrawing his arm from her grasp. He was still angry, but the fall had knocked some of the starch out of him.

"Come inside and get cleaned up."

As he started back toward the house, she kept in step with him, glancing back in hurt and bewilderment at Max.

"I'm leaving, Elizabeth."

Brodie spun around. "Good," he said smugly. "We don't need you around here, especially after you walked out on Mom and me."

As Liza Jane gasped, Max sensed the boy's slip of the tongue was intentional, his way to find out the truth.

"Max didn't walk out on anyone!" she exclaimed in a hushed

whisper, glancing nervously at the stoop where her young daughter stood with Bernice. "Where on earth did you get such an idea?"

"I heard talk around town."

"Kids say things they know nothing abou—"

"Not just kids. I overheard Paul's parents sayin' everybody knows you were with *him*"—His head jerked toward Max.—"right up until you married Dad. They talked about how your quick wedding surprised everyone. They always suspected Max left you pregnant and his best friend took the bullet for him."

Max nearly started a coughing fit over the absurd choice of words.

Liza Jane looked at Bernice and Annie, then turned her back to them and faced Brodie. "I am sorry you heard those rumors. They were wrong. I swear to you with all my heart that your dad is your biological father. I had hoped you would never find out what really happened, the mistakes I made. But I'm human, too. And you're old enough now to know the truth."

Elizabeth explained, as briefly as possible, the painful events of the past.

"I loved your dad, Brodie. Don't ever think I didn't. Yes, Max was part of my past. And that's where I left him after I married your father. But your dad was heartbroken to lose his best friend over what happened between us. They were as close as brothers. Maybe even closer."

"And now Dad's gone and you're going back to his best friend? Your old boyfriend? You know what everybody is going to think, don't you?"

She slowly nodded. "They'll think they were right all along—that Max really is your father."

"Yeah. How am I supposed to deal with that?"

"By knowing I've told you the truth and ignoring the gossip. Whether I marry Max or not, those rumors won't go away. As you grow up, you will realize you can't worry about what other people think as long as you know the truth for yourself."

Brodie looked at his mother, his eyes moist with unshed tears. Then he glanced warily at Max.

Elizabeth felt her heart breaking into a thousand tiny shards. She touched her son's arm. "Please don't make me choose between you."

His gaze darted from her to Max. After a long, tense silence, he finally said, "I guess you need to do whatever will make you happy again, even if it means getting married."

When she hugged him tightly, Brodie blushed with embarrassment, quickly excused himself and went inside, followed by Bernice and Annie.

Left alone with Elizabeth, Max wrapped his arms around her and pulled her close. As another rain shower began, he kissed her deeply, then pulled back and cupped her face in his hands. "Marry me."

She grinned. "Didn't we have this conversation already?"

"I said I'd make an honest woman of you. I never officially asked and you never officially answered. Will you marry me?"

"Yes!"

He kissed her again. "When?"

"Tomorrow?" Her eyebrows rose with wide-eyed excitement, then fell into a frown. "What about your mercy flights?"

"Pack your bags," he warned good-naturedly. "I'm not leaving you behind ever again."

"I don't know..." Her words trailed off as his lips pressed kisses down her neck. "I didn't handle the last trip too well."

"Give me one more chance." His warm breath against her skin sparked a fire in her. "Come with me. Right now."

"Where will we go?"

"You'll see."

She pulled back and gazed into his midnight-blue eyes. Raindrops clung to his dark lashes as he gave her a mischievous grin that sent a wave of excitement down to her toes.

"Trust me."

His two words teased her with a wicked enticement she couldn't resist.

～

WITHIN MINUTES, THEY WERE on their way to the Wilder farm. Within an hour they were airborne, flying north, breaking free of the storm front.

"How beautiful." Elizabeth stared past Max as she viewed the distant sunset through his side window.

"Yeah," he answered, gazing at her instead of the western horizon.

"You're looking in the wrong direction."

"Am I?"

"You're staring at me."

"I am?"

His penetrating eyes filled her with lusciously naughty thoughts, escalating her temperature one degree at a time. "Shouldn't you be watching where we're going?"

"Probably." His slow grin sizzled across the small space between them. The loud drone of the plane engines seemed to echo the hum of her own body. She tried to distract her wayward imagination by watching his hands on the controls. But she found herself recalling the gentle caress of those fingertips on her flesh.

With an almost inaudible moan, she turned her face toward her window, forcing her lungs to take a long, slow, deep breath. When he touched her arm unexpectedly, she nearly jumped from her seat.

"Come here." He had a gleam in his eye as he slid his chair

backward on its track. She glanced at the array of gauges, all of them maintaining a steady reading.

"Who's flying the plane?"

"Autopilot." He took her hand and tugged her to his lap. "Have I ever told you about the legendary Mile-High Club?"

"No..." Her heart tripped a beat as he reached for the top button of her blouse.

"It is an elite group of risk-taking adventurers who experience mind-blowing euphoria at high altitudes."

"A-are you sure you should be doing this?" She tried to avoid touching a knob or switch that might send them into a nosedive. "Isn't it dangerous?"

He chuckled, expertly stripping away her silk shirt and bra, leaving her wearing only her unzipped jeans. "Danger is half the fun of it."

"And the other half is...?"

"Your initiation into the club." His mouth covered hers, kissing her senseless while his hands peeled off the last remnants of her clothing. She anxiously unbuckled his belt and released him from the confining denim. With a minimum of movements, he shifted her position to straddle his hips.

Sheathing him to the full depth of her feminine core, Elizabeth felt as if his entire being had entered her body, filling her with his wild, untamed spirit. He unleashed his passion within her, igniting her own reckless desire.

"Welcome to the Mile-High Club, Liza Jane," he taunted breathlessly, his voice nearly lost beneath the sound of the powerful engines. She smiled, knowing he would tease her mercilessly in the days and years ahead. But it didn't matter. Nothing mattered now. She was too happy to care. Gloriously happy.

His hands grasped her hips as she climbed higher and higher toward the peak of her pleasure. She gripped his broad shoulders, cried out his name and carried him with her over the top of the clouds.

Afterward, tears streamed freely down her face. Her gaze fell upon the devilish tattoo on his bicep. Her fingertips traced the outline, then reverently touched the lettering of his youthful nickname. Smiling to herself, she lowered her lips to his, kissing him gently.

"Welcome home, Wildman."

TWO YEARS LATER, Bernice hosted a Labor Day barbecue fundraiser at the farm for the McKenzie Foundation for Women, which now had two facilities—the refurbished boarding house in downtown Alton and the Wilder farmhouse, both with security personnel. Max had contributed a significant sum of money to make the Foundation known to the public and offer more than shelter to women in need.

Although busy with her work as director, Bernice had just promised Max to spend part of the winter, including Christmas, with them on their ranch in Arizona, but only if they would come back to Alton for Easter and a good chunk of summer vacation.

Max smiled at his honorary mother-in-law. "That final decision is up to Elizabeth."

He scanned the crowd for his wife, spotting Brodie in his own battered cowboy hat, charming the socks off at least three high school girls. His stepson was a freshman at Arizona State University, hoping to continue in law school. Eleven-year-old Annie was giggling with a cluster of old girlfriends over lemonade and hamburgers. Like Brodie, Annie had taken to ranch life like a duck to water. She was one hell of a cowgirl. It was going to take considerable coaxing to get her to delay her rodeo dreams until after college.

When Elizabeth finally appeared in his field of vision in a soft peach skirt and white blouse, Max remembered the day she had walked through the open gate two years earlier. He felt a tug of desire at the sight of her full curves as she made her way to his side. Proud of her successful counseling to stabilize her weight, he kissed her lightly, then gently took the bundle in her arms.

Max gazed proudly down at the sleeping face of his three-month-old daughter. Careful not to wake her, he slowly lifted her tiny hand and gently kissed the back of it.

Elizabeth stood close to his side, looking up into his softened features. Unable to pull her gaze away from the two of them, she asked, "Bernice, did you ever imagine the day that Wildman Wilder would turn into Devoted Daddy?"

With a twinkle in her eyes, Bernice stood back and admired the three of them with a mile-wide grin. "Land sakes, child, I never doubted it for a minute."

Dear Reader,

In the summer of 1993, Romance Writers of America held the annual conference in St. Louis, Missouri. The hotel stood a short distance from the famous St. Louis Arch. Unfortunately, the Midwest was in the middle of one of the worst disasters—The "100-Year-Flood" aka *The Great Flood of '93*. Many writers cancelled their plans to attend the conference. Some of those in attendance told stories of watching from their hotel room windows, high above the Mississippi, as barges broke loose from their moorings and slammed into the bridge leading into the city.

After the conference ended, thirty or forty writers had planned an evening of dining and gambling aboard a floating casino in Alton, Illinois. While payment had been arranged months in advance, the cancellation policy did not address natural disasters, so no refund would be granted. That is, unless the writers made the request in person, which was still not a guarantee of recouping the significant loss of money. When a few of the original group decided to go ahead with their plans, one of them—Julie Hurwitz—invited me to fill one of the vacant seats on the bus.

Our bus driver had to go out of his way to find an accessible route, which was our first red flag. We drove over a long bridge that was only fifteen feet above the floodwater. Someone pointed to a half-submerged Wendy's fast-food sign—the type of sign perched on a tall twenty- or thirty-foot pole, high above the restaurant! The elevated road took us through mile after mile of brown waterscape dotted with the tops of trees and roofs of farm houses. The thirty-five-minute drive lengthened into six minutes, then ninety. At times, the bus drove through shallow water seeping through sandbag barriers. Members of our group grew more concerned, expressing their desire to turn around and go back. By the time we arrived in Alton, we intended to board the casino boat just to use the restroom, possibly get a sandwich supper to go, then hightail it back to St. Louis—with or without a refund.

Passing National Guardsmen patrolling the business district to protect from looters, the bus driver parked as close as possible to the permanently docked casino boat. However, we still had to walk a distance along the edge of the swollen river where it lapped at the sidewalk.

As I described in THAT WILDER MAN, a few men were trying to save an old brick building. The water was only a couple yards from the front door. Sandbags blocked our path. (Stepping on sandbags is a huge no-no!) To circumvent the barrier, we needed to go back to the street where the bus was parked, then climb a steep hill to go around the block.

The men saw our predicament and invited us to pass through their maze of sandbags, water hoses and lawn chairs, offering a helping hand to guide us. As we made our way over and around the obstacles, we apologized for our intrusion. One of the volunteers joked that we could contribute a percent of our winnings on our return.

I felt terrible about the assumption we were going to have an evening of fun entertainment when we only wanted to use the restroom and leave. (If ever there was an "accidental tourist," I certainly felt like one!) I paused to explain our awkward situation. Allowing my fellow writers to continue to the casino, I chatted with the gentleman who introduced himself as Sam Roberts and gave me his business card. Twenty minutes later, my group returned, carrying boxed dinners prepared for us by the kitchen staff of the casino.

The next day, *USA Today* ran a front-page photo of Alton, announcing the flood had crested the previous afternoon, August 1—the same time as our group had been there. I had chills. Not only had I witnessed the Great Flood, I had stood at the river's edge during a historical moment.

After I returned home, I wrote a letter to Sam, asking if the building had been saved. (It had.) However, the electrical facility had flooded, shutting down power to the town for more than a week. He finished with a PS: "Why don't you write a romance about a local guy manning the pumps during a flood who meets a sexy lady in jeans and cowboy boots? I laughed to myself. Yes, I happened to be wearing jeans and cowboy boots, but I certainly do not consider myself sexy!

Even though I had been writing historical romances and time-travel romantic suspense, I thought "Why not?" Thanks to Sam's suggestion, I wrote this contemporary romance with the working title of *Wet & Wilder*.

When I sent the book proposal to editors, I received rejections stating, *"A floo⚹ is too ⚹epressing for a romance novel."* or *"Sorry, the floo⚹ is past-history. No one wants to rea⚹ about something that will never happen again."* Each year, another devastating flood happened somewhere in the U.S., and I would wonder about the "past-history" nonsense. So I would send the book proposal again.

Four years after my trip to Alton, Harlequin Temptation published the manuscript with the new title, THAT WILDER MAN. I received letters from flood survivors who appreciated my realistic depiction of the disaster and the volunteers who worked so hard. Most of all, they enjoyed the positive and uplifting ending. I am very grateful to those readers who loved the book.

If you would like to see photos of the Great Flood of '93, they are available on my Pinterest page:

https://www.pinterest.com/SuePhillips_Author/That-Wilder-Man

I hope you enjoyed THAT WILDER MAN. If so, please consider helping to expand my readership by leaving a review at the point of purchase.

Thank you,
Sue

∿

Sue also writes award-winning time-travel romances, women's fiction and narrative non fiction. Turn the page for an excerpt of her latest women's fiction release: YOU OUGHTA KNOW

YOU OUGHTA KNOW

CHAPTER ONE

Pictures of new mothers holding their tiny babies covered half the wall of the examination room. Ten years ago, Megan Fisher had watched her photo go up on the bulletin board and had told Dr. Ames that she planned to add several more to his collection.

"At least eight kids," she had said.

"On a policeman's salary?" her doctor had asked. "Or is your husband still holding on to the hope of being the next Michael Connelly?"

"Writing is Stewart's dream. Mine is babies. Lots of them." She recalled the conversation while staring at the array of adorable babies. *At least one of us got our wish.* A twinge of sadness swept past her before her thoughts were interrupted by a deep, soft-spoken voice at the foot of the table.

"You probably only suffer from stress-related amenorrhea." Dr. Ames sat on the stool as he pulled on a pair of white latex gloves. His medical assistant silently stood by, waiting for him to begin his exam. "Not surprised either. It's probably hard enough being married to a detective, never mind a big-name author. I suppose he's either tracking down bad guys or writing about them."

"Or flying around the country to promote his latest novel." Her voice sounded a little too lighthearted, too cheery. "I don't mind. I've got a classroom of sixth graders to keep my mind from worrying about Stewart. But Jason misses the days when his dad was more available."

"Hard to believe I delivered your boy ten years ago."

Faintly aware of the doctor's movements, she let her eyes remain on the photos. The metallic click of instruments unnerved her. She tried to take a calming breath without being obvious. It was only an exam, for heaven's sake. Dr. Ames gave her no cause for this skittishness. Still, she hated this feeling of being so vulnerable.

"Despite your symptoms, there is no sign of pregnancy."

"But I'm over a month late. I've heard of IUDs failing at the end of their use."

"Yes, but stress is probably the reason for your missed periods. There are other choices for birth control." He paused, looking up. "Unless you're ready to have that little girl you've always wanted."

Megan forced a weak smile. "Stewart thinks we're too old to start over again."

"At thirty-three? Hardly. But if that's how he feels, he should make it permanent." Getting up from the stool, he peeled off the gloves and threw them away. "You can sit up now."

Clutching the paper gown, she made an awkward attempt until he took one elbow and steadied her, then stepped back and leaned against the counter, folding his arms across his chest. Dr. Ames was in his late thirties, with a California tan and a gentle manner that made most of his patients fall a little bit in love with him, including the white-haired ladies. Even Megan had entertained a small crush on him during her frequent office visits while expecting Jason.

"As soon as your body is back on track, the tenderness in your breasts and the edema will take care of themselves. Give it another month." He gave her a smile of encouragement that she tried to return. "Meanwhile, enjoy this heat wave we're having and take the rest of the day off. If I didn't have a full schedule, I'd be hitting the beach myself. Go home and relax—doctor's orders."

~

Several minutes later, Megan left the medical building near Memorial Hospital and drove her Lexus down the streets of Long Beach toward the ocean, turning from Second Street onto the narrow streets of her Naples Isle neighborhood. Her three-story house looked more like an Italian villa, towering over the sidewalks surrounding their pie-shaped corner lot one block from the circular canal.

Five years earlier on Christmas Eve, Stewart had given her a velvet jeweler's box. She had expected a ring. An emerald, hopefully. Her birthstone. Instead, she had found a house key tucked inside.

"To our new home," Stewart had said with the enthusiasm of a little kid, never realizing that she might have wanted to share in the enormous decision to buy a multimillion-dollar house.

But Stewart wasn't that way. He made decisions for himself, not her. Sometimes Megan wondered why she hadn't once questioned this behavior when they were dating. Back then, he joked about being her knight in shining armor, someone who wanted nothing more than to take care of her, slay her dragons, treat her like a princess. Never once had she considered that he was incapable of thinking of anyone else but himself.

Megan pulled into the garage, cut the engine, and punched the remote button, shutting out the afternoon sun. Tossing her keys into her purse, she tried to shake off the feeling of unease that had plagued her since this morning.

Her sixth-grade students had picked up on it, acting out more than usual before she had left for her appointment.

She dropped her head back against the headrest and closed her eyes, half wishing for a physical reason behind her symptoms. Something simple. Something treatable. Not cancer, God forbid. And definitely not a pregnancy.

Opening her eyes, Megan took a slow, deep breath and exhaled, wondering how Dr. Ames would have reacted if he'd known that her charming and handsome husband hardly noticed her in recent months, making love to her as if it was an appointment penciled into his busy schedule somewhere between calls from his personal publicist and emails from his editor.

Despite his notoriously sexy crime novels, Stewart left passion to the pages of his books. Not that her husband wasn't good in bed. On the contrary, he knew exactly how to satisfy her. His technique was flawless.

But completely devoid of emotion.

The words seemed to have a voice of their own, taunting her with the pathetic truth behind their perfect marriage. She'd loved Stewart almost from the first moment they had met in college. Even though he said he loved her, he was not the type to show it. Orphaned at fifteen, he'd shut down his emotions, which served him just fine in the police force, he'd once told her, firmly closing the door on the subject.

Get over it, Megan.

Mentally pushing aside the quiet loneliness, she went through the door leading into the kitchen. As she entered the house, she left her purse and school papers on the counter adjacent to the back stairwell, then paused at the first step to slip the high heels off her swollen feet. With shoes dangling from one hand, she slowly climbed the two flights to the third floor where the melody from a jazz saxophone drifted to her ears.

A renewed feeling of dread swept over her.

She slowed, listening.

Initially, she thought the music was coming from somewhere beyond the open windows at the end of the hall. But as she approached her bedroom, she heard a weather report, then another song being introduced.

It's only the clock radio, she realized with relief. She must have forgotten to shut it off in her morning rush.

Unbuttoning her silk blouse, she decided Dr. Ames was probably right about her stress level. If something as trivial as a radio could shoot her heart rate sky-high, she needed to learn how to relax. She would start with a nice long soak in the Jacuzzi tub, then curl up with a good book until Jason came home from school.

Struggling with the one-handed approach, she looked down at the stubborn button as she walked through the doorway.

Stewart's chuckle brought her head up. Across the room, the floral bedspread rippled and shifted with movement.

"Stewart?" His name rushed past her lips so softly Megan wasn't even sure she had spoken until she heard a muffled curse coming from the bed.

She watched him scrambling beneath the covers, tangling himself in the sheets. Panic etched his face as he glanced down at his partner, then back at her. Her gaze fell to his companion.

Recognition rocked her back on her heels. A cherished member of their extended family for longer than she could remember. Someone she trusted. Her trembling hand cupped her mouth as she stared at the one person she never dreamed would betray her in this way.

"Maxwell?

~

Stewart scrambled to sit up, throwing his legs over the edge of the bed, purposely blocking the view between his wife and his lover. "I know you're upset, Meggie, but—"

She held up her hand, momentarily halting his words. Her mouth moved, yet she didn't speak. Her eyes blinked back glistening tears.

"I'm sorry, Megan..." Ignoring his own nakedness, he went to her, but she backed away as if repulsed by the sight of his body. "Let me explain."

She shook her head, then turned and ran from the room.

Dashing to the other side of the bed for his pants, Stewart couldn't bring himself to look at Maxwell.

"What on earth are you going to say to her, Stew?"

"I don't know." He was having a hell of a time getting his foot through the pant leg. "I can't lose her though. Not now."

"It's too late, I'm afraid. For once in your life, you can't smooth talk your way around Megan. She'll leave you, you know."

"No, she won't." He finally got into his pants, zipped them, and grabbed a T-shirt from the floor. "I won't let her," he said, pulling the shirt over his head. "There's too much at stake. You know that as much as I do."

"You haven't much choice now."

"I will not walk out on my family like her father did. She never got over that. I'll talk to her. I'll explain."

"For God's sake, this is not as if she caught you with another woman. She can't very well forgive you just to avoid losing a father for Jason."

Stewart finally brought himself to glance at the man he had loved long before Megan had entered the picture. Maxwell had become a highly respected professor at the state university in town. Even though it didn't matter if anyone knew his sexual orientation, Maxwell kept his private life private. The last thing either of them wanted was a public scandal over their longtime relationship.

"Wait for me," he said, pausing at the threshold to make sure he was heard.

Bare-chested, the sheet draped discreetly at his waist, Maxwell shook his head solemnly. At thirty-nine, he had become only more distinguished with his salt-and-pepper hair and fine lines at the corners of his gray eyes. There was a gentleness in him unlike any man Stewart had ever known.

"I don't want to lose you," Stewart admitted.

Maxwell gave him a smile that might have been meant to be encouraging, but seemed more sad than anything else. In one instant their private paradise had been shattered. Nothing would be the same again.

"I'll find my way out without Meggie seeing me," Maxwell said.

Stewart nodded with resignation, then turned and raced toward the back stairs.

~

Megan had started to leave but made it only as far as the kitchen. Keys and purse in hand, she stared at the door to the garage, suddenly realizing she had nowhere to go. She couldn't fly to Florida and show up on her mother's doorstep. Not without Jason, anyway. And not without her son knowing something was desperately wrong. Besides, this wasn't something she could tell her mother, a crusty old woman embittered by her own ancient loss. She had refused to accept that Megan had found a man who wouldn't abandon her. Instead, her mother stayed away, even from her own grandchild.

Megan didn't have any close friends to take her in, except other teachers at school. Considering Stewart's notoriety as a famous author, the last thing Megan wanted to do was air their dirty laundry to someone outside the family. She couldn't risk it. One leak to the wrong person...

It wasn't Stewart she wanted to protect. Or herself. Jason was the one she needed to shelter from this ugly truth.

Images of her husband with Maxwell flooded her mind. Numb from the shock, she sat down hard on the last step.

Her own husband had been having sex with another man. The big-shot detective, the macho crime novelist, the man who declined marriage proposals from female fans on a weekly basis was living a lie. And she was caught in the middle of it.

How could she not have known? Especially about Maxwell?

"Megan?"

The sound of her husband's voice came from behind her. He was standing on the landing above, though she didn't turn to look at him. Instead, she clutched her purse to her chest and rose to her feet.

Stewart came down the stairs. "Where are you going?"

"Back to work," she said. Even if it was the truth, which it wasn't, she still wouldn't have been able to meet his gaze without seeing him and Maxwell together in bed. She reached for the doorknob.

"We need to talk."

"Jason will be expecting me."

"Not for two more hours." He reached for her arm. She pulled away. He reached again, slowly this time, taking the purse and placing it on the nearby counter. "Give me a chance to explain—"

His cool handling of her was too much for her to bear. She wasn't a murder suspect who needed to be worked by some compassionate detective. "How could you?" she demanded, her voice escalating. "Here! In our house? In our bed?"

"It's not like you to get hysterical, Meggie. Calm down."

"Don't tell me to calm down when I have every right to act any way I please. And for once in my life I'm not going to pretend to be your mild-mannered Megan. Damn it, Stewart, answer my question. How long? How many others besides Maxwell?"

"No one else. I swear that's the truth. As for Maxwell, it's just something that happened out of the blue. You and I both knew about his...background, so to speak. This afternoon he and I got to talking about it and, well, one thing led to another in our conversation and—"

"And I don't believe for one second that this...this *thing* with Maxwell just accidentally happened this afternoon." She was shouting now. It was the only way she could keep from dissolving into a mess of tears. "God damn you, Stewart. You owe me the truth."

"The truth is that I love you, Megan. I didn't do this to hurt you. I was curious. You know how I am. I'm a writer at heart. Always open to new experiences to enhance the writing."

"Bullshit."

His eyes registered shock. She never used such language. Ever.

"This isn't like going to a sushi bar for research, Stewart. Or scuba diving with sharks. Don't insult my intelligence."

His shoulders slumped. A minute ticked by as he stared forlornly at his feet.

"How long has this been going on?"

His head jerked up. His mouth opened and closed.

"How long?" she repeated.

He closed his eyes, unable to meet her angry gaze. "Fifteen... years." Her sharp intake of breath drew his eyes up in panic. "I made a mistake, Meggie. But I don't want to make the same mistake your father made. I don't want to disappear without a trace. I don't want to abandon you or Jason. Please forgive me."

Several mornings later, Megan reluctantly opened her eyes and glanced at the digital clock on the bedside table. She'd managed to finally fall asleep around sunrise, and now it was almost noon.

Dragging herself out of the bed in the guest room on the second floor, she went into the adjoining bathroom.

Avoiding her desolate reflection in the mirror was impossible as she methodically washed the sleep from her face. Her eyes were more red than brown, with dark circles beneath them. Her long brown hair was dull and tangled. She looked as bad as she felt.

The past few days were a blur, a self-induced fog of functioning on a normal level as a mother and a teacher, pretending nothing was wrong, while shutting out the sickening reality of the nosedive into hell that her life had taken.

As far as their son knew, his parents were sleeping on separate floors because of an unresolved argument, nothing more.

If only that was all this was about.

There was no argument to resolve. After Megan had discovered Stewart with Maxwell that afternoon, she'd barely heard him begging for her forgiveness. But nothing in the world could make her forgive. Or forget.

I wish I could forget.

But all she could do now was to pretend her perfect world was not shattered. She had to do it. For Jason's sake.

"Mom? Are you up yet? It's Sunday. Did you forget where we're going?" The soft voice of her ten-year-old came through the closed door of the bedroom. "We gotta be at the camp by two- thirty."

"I know, honey." She slipped into her pink cotton robe and cinched the sash at her waist, then picked up her hairbrush as she walked toward the door. "I'm running a little slow lately."

Brushing through her hair, wincing at the tangles, she opened the door to find him holding her coffee mug.

"Bless you, sweet child."

Her corny endearment widened his lopsided grin. Dressed in shorts and a T-shirt, he was starting to develop a deeper tan from the early summer sun.

As they walked over to the bed together, she sipped the coffee and sighed contentedly. "You remembered the cinnamon."

"Dad did it."

Her step faltered, and she nearly spilled the coffee. Stewart was supposed to be at a book festival in Denver the entire weekend.

"Your father's home already?"

Jason nodded. "He came back early 'cause of you. But he's sure you'll be feeling like your old self real soon."

"He said that, did he?"

Megan wondered how her husband could possibly believe that she could go back to being her "old self." Her old life was over. Their life as a family was over. But Stewart didn't see it that way at all, especially after she'd agreed to hold off telling their son of the inevitable divorce. Only temporarily though. Just for a few weeks. Just until school was finished for the year. Then she would tell him.

"Dad says until you're better I'm supposed to be extra good to you."

With the mug in one hand, she dropped the brush on the bed and reached out to him. "Jason, you are always extra nice to me. I couldn't ask for a better son. Please, honey, don't think that any of this is your fault. Your dad and I have some differences right now."

"Is that why you want to send me away for the summer?"

Her heart ached. "We're not *sending* you away. We're giving you a chance to have some fun rather than hanging out with boring grownups during your vacation. The Flying K Camp is supposed to be a terrific place, Jason. And the two of us will have a great time visiting it today. You'll see."

"Make that the *three* of us," added her husband, standing in the open doorway of the guest room.

"Stewart." Megan jumped up, sloshing the coffee over the rim of the cup and onto her robe. "What do you mean *three*?"

He slouched against the door jamb with his hands in his front pockets of his jeans. In his black blazer and white sports shirt, he could have been posing for his publicity photo on the back of his crime novels. Just as dark and moody too.

"I caught an early flight so I could tag along with you." He gave her the slight smile that his female fans found so sexy. So had she. Now it reminded her of how easily she had been fooled by him for so long.

"Cool, Dad!"

Megan turned to their son. "Jason, take my cup to the kitchen, please. Your father and I need to talk."

After a minor protest from his son, Stewart stepped forward. "Do what your mother asked, Jase."

"Yes, sir." Scuffing his bare feet on the white carpet as a final show of disgruntlement, he left the room.

When he disappeared from view, Megan closed the door and turned to her husband. "You're not going with us, Stewart."

"Let's not fight, Meggie." Despite his placating tone, an undercurrent of warning emanated from him.

"Don't do this." Closing her eyes and covering her ears, she wished she could make him disappear. Better yet, make their entire life together disappear. Except for Jason.

"I'm still his father," he said softly as if talking to a child. He lightly grasped her arms, but she shook him off, unable to bear his touch. "I don't intend to be shut out of his life. We can work this out if only you would—"

"Stop it, Stewart." She retreated to the far side of the room before turning to look at him again. She fought to control the quiver in her voice but failed. "How can you possibly expect me to put aside my feelings, my hurt, my anger at you? I can't possibly act as if nothing has happened."

"But you can't walk out on me. Not now. What about all we worked for?"

She had always known he was the center of his own universe.

But blaming her for the damage he'd done to their marriage was more than she could take.

"Leave. Now."

He didn't move. Instead, he watched her in silence.

"If you don't go downstairs and tell Jason that you have a sudden emergency and have to leave, I'll tell him about Maxwell."

"You'd never do that."

She was bluffing and she knew he knew it. There was no way she would ever reveal the truth to Jason. Not the whole story, anyway. Not about finding his father in bed with his beloved Uncle Maxwell. But she had no other cards to play. With any luck, Stewart would back down. She counted on it.

"I never said 'never,' only later. But I won't tolerate your Happy Threesome charade. It's only going to make it that much harder on Jason when he finally learns the truth."

His eyes narrowed. "This isn't over, Megan."

No, of course not. It would never be over. But at least she'd won this particular standoff.

As he closed the door behind him, she leaned back against the wall to steady herself. She could feel the drop of adrenaline like the sudden free fall of an elevator. Her knees weakened and buckled. Slowly she slid down the wall until she sat on the floor.

And the tears came again.

Two hours later, driving north along the congested Pacific Coast Highway through Malibu, Megan regarded her son's silence with an edge of concern. She attempted to carry on a conversation with Jason, but it was mainly one-sided.

She knew he was disappointed that his father hadn't come along with them. Stewart had waited until the last minute before backing out, claiming he'd forgotten about some important business he needed to tend to. At least he hadn't blamed her for his change in plans. But then, she also saw how easily he'd fabricated the lie. He sounded so believable, so honest. How many times had she looked into those brown eyes and been more than willing to accept his excuses for working late, for not coming home to her?

She glanced at Jason.

He had changed in the last several months, withdrawing into sullen silences. Could he have already found out about his father's relationship with Uncle Maxwell, the man he'd known his entire life as if he was the patriarch of their little family?

She thought about the previous weeks, trying to remember if ever there had been a time when Jason might have come home unexpectedly from a friend's house and stumbled across a similar scene with his father as Megan had done.

She hoped not.

Her eyes focused on the northbound traffic on the highway. Certainly she would have sensed his anguish over something as huge as this. She didn't want to believe she could have missed the signs of such a traumatic experience.

She didn't believe his recent mood swings were severe enough to cause alarm, but then what did she know? She hadn't known about Stewart.

No, that was a bolt out of the blue. Or was it?

God, she was so confused. And hurt. Her whole world was shattered, and yet she'd forced herself to act as if nothing was wrong. For Jason's sake. Maybe even for her own.

She'd returned to her sixth-grade classroom to wrap up the final weeks before the end of school. But it'd been so hard to focus on anything. Nearly impossible.

Her son's silence this past week mirrored the tension at home with Stewart, not to mention her own anxiety over the tests she'd taken on Friday to find out if she'd contracted any diseases from her husband.

Her gut clenched as she thought about the possibility of an

STD. Yet if she spent too much time dwelling on it, she would crack. And she had to be strong for her son.

Despite Stewart's reassurance that he had been careful, she would be holding her breath until she heard from Dr. Ames. Her fingers immediately tightened on the steering wheel as she fought back the shocking image of her husband in their bed.

"Slow down, Mom! You're going to miss the turnoff."

Jason pointed out the pitted metal sign for Yerba Buena Road. A mile beyond the Los Angeles county line, the narrow two-lane road looked like all the others that branched off the coast highway into the Santa Monica Mountains.

"Thanks, honey." She reached over and lightly patted his shoulder. His head snapped around. His body tensed. But as quickly as he'd reacted, he relaxed.

Megan frowned. *What was that all about?*

Jason gave her a grin that was halfway between forced and genuine, as if to say, *I'm okay. Let's forget about it. Please?*

Megan hoped her own reassuring smile was more convincing.

~

To learn how to purchase this book, go to:
https://suephillipsauthor.com/books/you-oughta-know

BOOKS BY SUE PHILLIPS

Novels

YOU OUGHTA KNOW
(Contemporary Women's Fiction)
MYSTIC MEMORIES
(Time-Travel Romance Romantic Suspense)
THIS TIME TOGETHER
(Time-travel Romantic Suspense)
THAT WILDER MAN
(Contemporary Romance)
DARK COVENANT
(Paranormal Victorian Romantic Suspense)

True Crime with Deanne Acuña

LOSING LISA
Intuitive Investigator Series, Book One
FINDING FAYE
Intuitive Investigator Series, Book Two

ABOUT THE AUTHOR

Award-winning author **Sue Phillips** has been a college radio DJ and an aerobics instructor at Richard Simmons' *Anatomy Asylum*. She has counted whales as a member of the Gray Whale census and volunteered at the Cabrillo Aquarium as a Whale Watch Naturalist on board sea excursions off the coast of Southern California.

Published under various pseudonyms by St. Martin's Press, Berkley/Jove Books and Harlequin Enterprises, she is currently reissuing her previous novels through Sweetbriar Creek Publishing Company. She is a member of Novelists, Inc., Women's Fiction Writers Association, Alliance of Independent Authors and Romance Writers of America.

For more information about Sue, please visit:

https://suephillipsauthor.com
https://www.facebook.com/SuePhillipsAuthor
http://TWITTER.com/SuePhillips_
https://www.pinterest.com/SuePhillips_Author/